THE CLARKE COUNTY DEMOCRATS

A NOVEL OF LOVE, LIFE AND BASEBALL

PHIL BRADY

iUniverse LLC
Bloomington

THE CLARKE COUNTY DEMOCRATS
A NOVEL OF LOVE, LIFE AND BASEBALL

iUniverse books may be ordered through booksellers or by contacting:

iUniverse
1663 Liberty Drive
Bloomington, IN 47403
www.iuniverse.com
1-800-Authors (1-800-288-4677)

Because of the dynamic nature of the Internet, any web addresses or links contained in this book may have changed since publication and may no longer be valid. The views expressed in this work are solely those of the author and do not necessarily reflect the views of the publisher, and the publisher hereby disclaims any responsibility for them.

Any people depicted in stock imagery provided by Thinkstock are models, and such images are being used for illustrative purposes only.

Certain stock imagery © Thinkstock.

ISBN: 978-1-4759-9311-0 (sc)
ISBN: 978-1-4759-9312-7 (e)

Library of Congress Control Number: 2013909651

Printed in the United States of America.

iUniverse rev. date: 8/20/2013

CLARKE COUNTY DEMOCRATS

Pitcher	Cassity
Catcher	Constable
First base	Mister Shaw
Second base	Medicine Men
Shortstop	Medicine Men
Third base	Doctor Pearlington
Left field	Questionable
Center field	Arceneaux
Right field	Fingers
bench/reserves	Buckles
	Cobb
	Richie
Manager	Harrigan
Business manager	William Harold the Third
Owner/sponsor	George Washington's
	All American Stores

ROAD GAME, 1921

THEY STOLE THE BUS A year ago last December.

Between Christmas and New Year's Doctor Pearlington, the town pharmacist and third baseman, drove the others to Selma and dropped them off at the bus station.

They caught a bus to Montgomery and in Montgomery another to Atlanta. In Atlanta they took a third bus ride, this to the small town they had read about in the *Montgomery Advertiser*. The article had also carried a picture, the caption underneath saying "Chalucca School District sports first school bus." They walked a half-mile to the school.

"It's a godsend," the article quoted Ezra Titus, superintendent of the district, in pointing out the rarity of a small rural school district having its own school bus. "Now our little tykes won't have to walk to school. They will be picked up and dropped off."

In the small quiet town asleep early Sunday the two men walked a half-mile to the school.

School had let out for the holidays, so there was no one in the way. The bus sat behind the building. It was painted canary yellow. The two looked inside.. Four rows of wood seats on each side of an aisle. Perfect.

So the two walked back to town and Win Harrigan kicked in the back door of a hardware store. They stole two gallons of porch green and two paint brushes and walked the half-mile back to the school, where they painted the bus porch green. Now they had to start it.

"Crank?" asked Win Harrigan.

Constable, the second member of the party, went back in and rummaged behind the driver's seat. "Here," he said and held up the tool. "I'll get it going."

"Careful," said Win Harrigan, "these Macks can backfire. Break your arm".

"As many of our soldiers in France learned," Constable said.

"Gas?" asked Win Harrigan.

Constable found a yardstick behind the driver's seat. He ran the stick into the tank and told Win Harrigan they would need gas. The only gas station in town was closed because it was Sunday, and that suited them fine.; that was what they wanted.

Constable was called that because he was the Clarke County constable. Constable broke open the back door of the gas station and located the key which would unlock the pump. Constable knew every kind of key ever made, and he had the pump unlocked in half a minute. They filled up.

Constable looked around the station and found a five-gallon gasoline can. They filled that. They would need more on the way back to Thomasville but they could either buy some or rob another gasoline station. They weren't worried; the Clarke County Democrats had now acquired a bus.

The acquisition of a bus had done wonders for the spirits and the financial success of the Clarke County Democrats, the semi-professional hometown team of Thomasville, in west Alabama. Win Harrigan, owner and playing manager, sat behind the wheel. Not every town could boast a man like him, who'd made a commitment to baseball, who understood that baseball could power a vision.

Semi-professional meant the players were paid only for their expenses and weren't given any kinds of contracts. They earned their livings at other kinds of jobs.

With the bus, the Democrats became more than an effort at town boosterism, the team became a moneymaker.

The bus, built as an army vehicle, had been destined to do war duty in France. But that role had been intercepted by the Armistice in 1918 and it never left the U.S. and had been converted into a bus.

Having the bus meant that William Harold the Third, the Democrats' team business manager, unaware of the bus's illicit history, otherwise the vice president and chief accountant at the highly reputable State Bank of Clarke County, could write letters to baseball teams as far as a hundred miles away in order to schedule games. The Democrats could play as far away as Tuscaloosa or Selma; or Tupelo or Columbus or Waynesboro or Meridian.

Baseball was good for business. Baseball was about progress.

In such events, the Democrats took forty per cent of the gate, no expenses.

And so the Clarke County Democrats went on the road.

○

Today at one they would play a game against the Hibbett Grain and Silos team of Tupelo. The Democrats had to win this game, but by less than two runs.

Last year, the 1920 season, they had been able to increase the schedule from four to seven games. Out of town games. This year, William Harold the Third had put together a schedule of twelve games, eight out of town. The bus passed one of the team's posters. The poster featured manager Win Harrigan "in relaxed pose," as William Harold the Third described it in the letters to opposite business managers, standing at the steps of a dugout. Now that they had money, the Democrats could furnish up to fifty of these posters to promote a game.

The home team was supposed to take the posters to their local job printer and have him add the date and the time and the location, then nail the posters in key locations around town.

This poster of Win Harrigan "in relaxed pose" was nailed to a telephone pole.

SINGLE GAME
SUNDAY AFTERNOON 1 P.M.
BATTALION FIELD
CLARKE COUNTY DEMOCRATS VS. HIBBETT SILOS

Publicity. Good. The prospects of a good crowd.

Everyone had made the trip except Questionable. But then, Questionable didn't make every trip. No one even knew where Questionable lived. Sometimes he showed up. Sometimes he didn't. No one ever knew. His real name was Cousins. William Harold the Third had grown so used to Cousins not showing up he began to put a question mark after his name. Once he turned in the lineup card to the opposing scorekeeper with the word "questionable" on the card where Cousins' name was supposed to be. The scorer walked around the stands with a megaphone announcing the lineup to the spectators and called out "questionable" to the people in the stands.

William Harold the Third afterward put down "questionable" on the lineup card. Sometimes he simply put down a question mark.

Everyone else was on the bus. Win Harrigan owned and managed the team and drove the illicit bus. Win Harrigan had also made what the two, he and Aaron Silverstein, called "the arrangement". Not everyone on the team knew about "the arrangement," however, just a few knew how to make it work but certainly not William Harold the Third.

William Harold the Third sat in the seat behind the driver and Mister Shaw sat opposite William Harold the Third. Mister Shaw played first base and was also the principal at the Institute. People locally did not know exactly what purpose the Institute served. Individuals could be seen walking around on the grounds and some townspeople were hired for domestic work but why people were there was a mystery. Mister Shaw came to town for his civic club's meeting but never talked much about his job. In the seat behind William Harold the Third sat Constable, the catcher.

Constable had taken his catcher's glove apart and was working two upholsterers' tacks into the leather of the thumb from behind. Constable could draw a baseball across the tacks and create very fine, nearly invisible gashes in the leather. Any pitch thrown after that would perform some very funny wiggles and dances on its way to the plate. Another tack used for the same purpose he had already worked through his belt at the right hip. Constable felt no qualms about doing this because he knew the opposing pitcher had probably secreted an emery board somewhere on himself, or had combed a jar of Vaseline into his hair.

Of course if Leonard was pitching he never used the tacks. If Win Harrigan put himself into the game sometimes as pitcher, he would do it. Or if he put, God forbid, Fingers on the mound as a reliever, then he *had* to do it.

Across from Constable sat Doctor Pearlington the pharmacist, who also owned the Western Union franchise in town. Any telegram into or out of Thomasville went through Pearlington's Pharmacy. Doctor Pearlington relayed the arrangements. He played third base and took care of aches and pains.

Behind Constable were Medicine Men. Medicine Men were identical twins full-blooded Choctaw Indians. They played second base and shortstop, interchangeably, and in any inning no one could tell which of them was playing which position. They were the reason Win Harrigan considered asking Aaron Silverstein to steal him a set of uniforms with numbers on them. In these modern times *some* teams had started to put numbers on player uniforms, but it was a matter of finding a set going out of the warehouses in the right colors: a combination of red, white, and blue.

At home games Medicine Men brought with them a small bag of sticks. They piled the sticks behind second base and lighted them into a fire, then sat cross-legged before the fire and prayed to the Baseball King.

Buckles, did not like the ritual. He threatened that one day while they were out there daydreaming he would cut their throats.

Years ago an ancestor of Buckles' had been scalped by the Creeks. Medicine Men knew far more about this event than they let on. Anytime Buckles referred to the scalping Medicine Men simply looked at each other and rolled their eyes.

Mister Harrigan said to Buckles, that, first, he was so stupid he did not know which out to make first in a double play and had proven that fact several times over, and Medicine Men did know which out to make first, and, second, this was America, and "it is next to impossible to find a good shortstop in America," and if he did attempt that he would string Buckles up himself without waiting for a trial.

Fingers, the church organist who did not like Buckles, overheard Mister Harrigan say this and told Buckles "why don't you go light your own Goddamn fire."

This had happened, Fingers saying that, last game. Buckles did not like Fingers' comment and had found a way to get even. Doctor Pearlington always brought with him a bag which contained salves and pills, tape and bandages, iodine and what-not to deal with minor scrapes and sprains. Included in the bag was a jar of analgesic balm, a thick salve made from chili peppers, to be rubbed on muscle aches and pains. It turned the skin warm, even hot, where applied. Often *very* hot.

Buckles had found a way to get into Doctor Pearlington's bag and had transferred a large dollop of analgesic to Fingers' athletic supporter... Now he sat in the back of the bus grinning in satisfaction, knowing Fingers was playing right field in agony as his testicles turned red.

Medicine Men had begun to bring their bag of sticks to games away from home. Mister Harrigan did not want to forbid the practice but he cautioned Medicine Men not to attract too much attention to it. "Just use small sticks," he told them.

Toward the rear of the bus sat the outfielders and the utility man, the previously mentioned Buckles. Fingers and Bonehead Arceneaux crowded into one seat. Fishpond "Bonehead" Arceneaux aristocrat French ancestors had founded the town of Demopolis, "The City of the People," in Alabama. They were refugees and incompetent as farmers. At Demopolis they had hoped to produce wine and olives, just as their ancestors did on their estates in the old days in the old country. But the colony failed and now only Bonehead was descended from it, a kind of punk keepsake in Alabama of its French heritage.

Bonehead played center field. Fingers, his seatmate, taught piano and filled in at churches as an organist. He could play almost any instrument. Sometimes he ran his fingers across the thigh of the player on the seat next to him, and so he almost always ended up sitting alone. Bonehead made his living setting out trotlines for catfish in the Tombigbee River and, when he could get his hands on dynamite, dynamiting catfish.

He had a small cache leftover from one time when a timber company cleared pine forest and then dynamited the stumps to send to the gunpowder works in Mississippi. The war overseas ended and the gunpowder demand died off, and so Bonehead helped himself to the dynamite shed. But the stuff was old now and some of it would go off when it didn't need to, sometimes going off a little soon as far as Bonehead was concerned. Bonehead just never paid Fingers any attention.

In the last seats were Richie, Cobb and Buckles. Richie finished high school this year and he loved the game. Buckles drove a tractor, and Win Harrigan sent him to the plate only when it was absolutely necessary for a Democrat to strike out. Now that the Democrats were fixing games for the sake of gamblers it became necessary at times not to score too many runs. Buckles could not hit a fish swimming in a rain barrel with a shotgun, as the saying went, but he could strike out convincingly. So Win Harrigan put him in at crucial times.

At other times he took care of the gear.

Cobb worked at the sawmill with Leonard.

Sprawled across the wooden bench at the rear was the pitcher, Leonard Cassity.

Leonard had a low kick that had never been taught him by anybody. It was fluid and as natural to him as taking a breath. It made for a deceptive stride, innocent and free. Free of ill will toward the hitter, toward the world. But it brought all the energy in his body, of a hundred and fifty pounds of intestine and sinew and bile and snot, through his shoulders and into his arms and wrists, where in turn it was transmitted by means of a vicious snap of the wrist into the leather sphere of a baseball.

At the plate, sixty feet and six inches away, it would suddenly leap from its letter-high plane straight up, six inches up, a jump as high as the batter's eyes. No one could stay away from it, but it was moving at probably one hundred miles an hour and only the most athletic of an opponent could lay a bat on it.

Leonard could throw this pitch for inning, after inning, and, if necessary, for hours. Leonard Cassity had fulfilled God's design for a baseball pitcher. Even God would probably have gasped at the beauty of him.

As usual, Leonard was hurting.

Doctor Pearlington made his way back to Leonard's bench.

"How you feeling, Leonard?" he asked.

"My bellyache, you know, Doc. You got anything? Maybe some Syrup of Black Draught or some Sal Hepatica?"

"Both bad, Leonard," said Doctor Pearlington. Give you the runs. Maybe during the game. Why don't I give you some Wrigley's Spearmint? It steadies the nerves. It's known for that."

"Yes, sir."

Doctor Pearlington went forward and came back. Leonard unwrapped the whole package. "You've got a lot to do today," said Doctor Pearlington.

"Yes, sir," said Leonard.

Up front, Win Harrigan asked how Leonard was. "Hypochondria, as usual," said Pearlington. "I gave him some chewing gum."

The game got underway. The two managers met at home plate and exchanged lineup cards. The home manager explained that the hay rake parked down the left field line was part of the playing field and a ball that rolled into it was still in play. The two umpires were in no mood for arguments. Their ordinary jobs were supervising a chain gang out at the prison farm.

The visiting Democrats went down in the first, one, two, three.

The chewing gum did not steady Leonard's nerves.

Leonard hit the first batter he faced; just grazing the letters on his chest, but the umpire awarded first base. Then Leonard walked two batters on eight pitches, including two curves that hit a foot in front of home plate and sent Constable scrambling. The Dems ought to be at least four runs better than this team. Many people had actually placed bets that the Democrats would be four runs better, or more. But under "the Correction, the "Arrangement," or the "Correct Score" worked out between Win Harrigan and Silverstein, the Dems would win today by two runs or less.

To Constable it began to look like the team may not win that day; it could lose—and by a lot more than two runs.

Constable called time, took off his mask and walked to the mound. "Leonard," he said, "if you walk one more batter I'll come out here and whip your ass." He spat on the ground and turned around. "Yes, sir," said Leonard to his back.

Leonard threw a fast ball that the batter was a mile behind. He threw a ball and then two more fastballs that made deadly buzzing sounds as they came across, like they were rattlesnakes.

Two more batters struck out on six pitches. No more curves. Just fastballs at the letters that jumped up in the eyes. No runs. No hits. No errors. Three men left on base.

ONE

"How'd you know my name?"

"It's Frances, ain't it?

"How'd you know?"

"That man outside told me. I asked him."

The girl saw a man in rubber boots outside the window. As the girl peered out the window the man peered in.

"My Daddy," she said. "Well, can I help you?"

"Ice cream cone."

"What flavor?"

"What's here?"

"Just vanilla. But if you want chocolate I can put some syrup on it."

"Chocolate."

"Five cents, please."

She was not pretty. Skinny. The dress hung a little loose. A bit of a pug nose. Nothing like the long elegant noses that belonged to the beauties she saw in the movies. Hair not brown but not blonde either. Off her shoulders but a bit of it on her forehead... She looked like the kind of girl who would finish last in the race at school no matter how much encouragement she got from her teammates. "Hurry, Frances!" called her best friend Mary Ann Ferguson. And Frances flagged on.

Frances was a plain girl from a plain town in West Alabama. She tended the counter in the summertime at her father's ice cream shop in Thomasville. Like the ice cream, a vanilla kind of a girl.

Leonard went into his pocket and out came several nickels. "Want one, too?" he asked. Frances gave him a sideways glance.

"Well, not while I'm working. My Daddy doesn't like me to do that."

"I'll buy it and you can eat it after work. Right there out front. I'll sit and watch you do it."

And so Leonard Cassity met Frances Smith.

"And you ain't got nothin' better to do than that?" she asked.

"Not until Monday. That's when I have to be at the sawmill over by Tallahatta."

"You lumber man?"

"Will be. Came up from Mobile to make lumber my career. Big future in it..."

"Mister Big Timber, huh?"

"What about you, Frances?"

"You don't know me well enough to call me Frances. You call me 'Miss what-my-last-name is'."

"What is your last name?"

"I'm not tellin' you."

"Your Daddy owns this here ice cream store?"

"Not just ice cream. All sorts of dairy products. Milk, cream. The milk is pasteurized. Delivers, too."

"Well, maybe I'll buy some milk, too. If you'll tell me your last name."

"Well, Smith, I guess."

"You guess it's Smith?"

"It's Smith. What size milk you want?"

"I think I don't have time to figure it out. I have to find a hotel. Some place for tonight."

"There's one over the drugstore. For when they come to buy the timber."

"Can I come back some time and buy you another ice cream?"

"Can if you have a nickel. Now you know my name but what is your name?"

"Leonard. Leonard Cassity."

○ ○ ○

Frances' father patiently let the courtship proceed and observed it with a touch of amusement. When Leonard was around, Mister Smith came into the front from the creamery behind and shooed Frances outside so she could eat ice cream with Leonard. Mister Smith then did the chores that Frances ought to have done. He swept the pine board floors and wiped the smudges from children's fingers off the glass ice cream case and he washed and put away the metal scoops. They spent their Saturday afternoons on the sidewalk outside her father's store in Thomasville, Alabama, Leonard and Frances did, eating cones of ice cream that melted in the West Alabama heat and ran down their fingers and making them sticky, puzzled by the vast and mysterious depths of one another's eyes, uncomprehending.

A few weeks before the wedding Mister Smith drove the couple out to the house he found for the couple to rent, two miles west of town at what was called Tallahatta Springs. Tallahatta had never had more than a collection of about five occupied houses. Now it had none occupied, and the houses sat scattered around, not any of them visible to the other. The house Mister Smith found was a little larger than the others, but just as decrepit.

"It belonged to some people who moved here from Virginia in the old days and then moved north to Tuscaloosa," he explained.

It, the house, sat on a red clay knob looking over a barely cleared patch of ground, but it was a grand house in its way. Spacious. Gray, mortared chimneys rose outside on either side, and the second floor had two windows on each side, and the porch was deep. The house had never been painted, and the pine clapboards had darkened into a somber brown, a brown Mister Smith compared to the seat of a well worn saddle.

The house had one of those Atlantic states spraddle roofs, broken gables at front and rear, not like those straight-roofed Creoles, whose roofs descended straight from the peak to the edge of the porch, but which angled off from the main roof to cover the porches.

"It's lovely," she said.

The angle provided by the spraddle made the front porch a delightful place, more than ten feet deep, probably twelve feet. Even now that the weather was hot the porch was not hot. It was shady, and the length of it seemed to capture any little movement of air. The porch offered up little breezes that belonged to Frances and to no one else. Frances imagined tucking herself way up to the wall in a chair out of the sun or the rain to shell peas or quilt or mend or read the Scriptures.

"Well's out here," he said, taking her to the pump half way between the house and the smokehouse combined with storage shed. "I'll bring you water."

Inside he worked the window sashes. "Now this here window," he pulled and struggled, "is stuck a little bit but that don't matter none because this here's the dining room." The window would not close any closer than two inches from the sill. Leonard worked on it many times in the first few months. He rubbed and rubbed candle wax inside the sash but the window would never move the last two inches. Finally Frances bought a newspaper in town and rolled it and pushed it into the open space. "Paper's a wonderful insulator, Leonard, did you know that?" she told him.

But that was the only one she ever worked on. It turned out that all the other windows were stuck, too. Some would not open; others would not close. Most sat at distinct angles from the frames.

Leonard settled on the rent down at the bank, which managed the property. Five dollars a month. Two days later Mister Smith drove them both to the house and Leonard gave Frances the grand tour.

They were married nine months later, one day after Frances's nineteenth birthday at the Methodist church where her uncle, Mister Smith's brother, was the exhorter. The exhorter knew little or no theology. He simply urged people to pray. He exhorted the guests to pray for this couple. Leonard was twenty.

They got married at a big brown Methodist church, When she told her mother she wished to marry, her mother said "will you let your cousin Amy be maid of honor?"

"Her? Not Fergie?"

"Yes, *her.*"

"I suppose."

Frances knew that Amy was the daughter her mother wished she'd had. And that was all there was to it. No one spoke of it as a family rivalry. Frances' mother married Sheldon Smith, who had attended the Alabama Polytechnic Institute at Auburn and studied agriculture then established the dairy. Her brother founded the local telephone exchange after he graduated from the University of Alabama at Tuscaloosa. Both succeeded, but no one in the family made comparisons as to their relative successes, and difficulties.

〇 〇 〇

Even before she was saved in the revival Frances sat by the wall and read the Scriptures. She liked the Book of Ruth. Ruth told Naomi "Wherever you go I shall go. Wherever you lodge I shall lodge. Your people shall be my people and your God, my God. Wherever you die I shall die and there shall I be buried beside you."

I am going to be that kind of daughter to Leonard's mother, Frances told herself.

But even after she was saved the Scriptures could not stop her from hating her mother-in-law, her personal Naomi, only that she was not the Naomi that Frances yearned for.

Her efforts to tolerate Leonard's mother came from God, a lesson from a page of inerrant scripture. That was all it was. A .lesson in Christian forgivenes Her hate for Leonard's mother continued from inside her. She wished that God could make a difference within her toward Leonard's mother.

At home a week before the wedding, as she prepared to leave home for the farm at Tallahatta, she went into her mother's old trunk. She had outgrown the tea parties a long time ago, she couldn't remember when now, but was it when she was around seven or eight? Why had her mother kept that little girl dress?

She picked up the poke bonnet as it lay near the bottom, the soft feel of it helping to bring up the memories of those days as a child and asking herself if that child had now become a woman. She tied its ribbons into a bow and set it out in front of her. "Frances," she said to the imaginary little girl under the bonnet, "are you ready for this?" Frances smiled a little girl smile at her showing big teeth. She put the bonnet into her new suitcase.

While Leonard was at work she would have Tallahatta Springs to herself.

And tying the poke bonnet to her head she sometimes took a basket out to "the acres" she called them, setting up a tea party for herself by spreading a gingham tablecloth across "Mister Low". After a few times the table cloth became sticky with bleeding resin and she found the stickiness hard to wash away. She stopped.

○ ○ ○

Frances had lots of other relatives on the big, broad lawn in front of the church. Aunts, cousins including Amy, her other uncle; many more relatives than Leonard. His mother had not put a large number on the guest list. "It's a long way to travel just for that," she told Leonard, whose feelings were a little hurt. But he did understand that it was a long way to travel. Leonard thought he was lucky that one of the Busby's from the Busby Brothers Yard saw fit to attend.

The bride's side and the groom's side eyed one another from opposite ends of the punch table, and from little clusters of guests around the lawn. Thomasville was giving up one of its prizes to a young stranger. Mrs. Cassity decided she would speak little to Mrs. Smith. Frances and Leonard stood mostly by themselves the whole reception. But with the exception of Fergie. Fergie stood next to Frances and smoothed her hair and protected her and brought her everything she asked for. Frances saw nothing except the radiant world she lived in. Her face, her eyes, her bearing, her smile radiated. Leonard was simply struck by this creature he had that day made his own.

Afterward her father dropped them off in his dairy truck at the spraddle-roof farmhouse not quite a mile from the sawmill where he worked, and Frances filled it with quilts and dishes and everything she could think of to do. Leonard set out on foot to his job barking pine logs at the Busby Brothers Yard and to his career in the lumber business.

○ ○ ○

When Frances was a girl her mother had sometimes fetched Frances' grandmother's old poke bonnet from a chest. Her mother made a gift of it to Frances, and then she would sometimes tie it around Frances' head and set up a tea party for Frances on the front porch. Now Frances did that again.

Sometimes Frances tied the poke bonnet to her head and took a basket out to "the acres" as she called them—a stretch of red Alabama clay punctuated all over by dark pine stumps. The land had been timbered years back but had struggled to re-grow.. More dense pine woods began again in the distance, far off at the point where the cleared forty acres ended. The tree stumps close to the house had never been pulled, and that would have let the land be given over to agriculture. So Frances wandered among acres of pine stumps and she made friends with them and gave them names. "Mister Frazzletop," and "Mister Armaround" for a stump that had a crooked root, "Mister Low" and "Mister Unhappy" for a grumpy stump. She spread a gingham tablecloth across "Mister Low." After a few times the tablecloth became sticky with bleeding resin, and she found the stickiness hard to wash away. She stopped.

When they had been married three months Frances said, "Leonard, do we want to go to Mobile to visit your Momma and your Daddy this weekend?"

"Ain't any way to get there."

"Found one out. It's my daddy has to go to Mobile to take a machine that helps to sterilize the milk bottles. It's got itself in a puny way. He's taking it Friday night. They're going to work on it Saturday and bring it back Sunday."

"Ummnnn." Leonard dried a dish.

"Mister Cammack's colored man is coming by Thursday to help him load it.

Frances and Leonard went to Mobile.

Leonard father had been hired to superintend the construction of the new paper mill, and Mister Cassity could now afford a brick home in one of the newer subdivisions. Mrs. Cassity found a better church to belong to and joined a study club. Men Mister Cassity did not know shook hands with him after church.

Frances found the Cassity's back yard a comfortable place. She offered to help Mrs. Cassity with the dishes Mrs. Cassity said no thank you and turned away, and so Frances went out the back door to the yard.

I'm the daughter-in-law, aren't I? I know how to be that. Why shouldn't I help?

For a little while she looked at the azaleas and the shrubs she'd never seen, imagining that she would plant a flower bed just like that one over there in Tallahatta. It was quiet there, just Frances by herself, and she did not want to interrupt Leonard's visit with his parents. Mrs. Cassity was icy toward her.

Late Saturday Frances came quietly through the screen door and thought she heard voices from the dining room. At the little butler's pantry between the kitchen and the dining room she stopped because Leonard and his mother seemed to be in earnest conversation.

"You could have done much better, Leonard," she heard Mrs. Cassity say. "Who is she? A milkman's daughter? Leonard replied in a low tone which Frances couldn't make out. "We know bankers now. And other prominent people. Why didn't you wait? I wish now you had never gone into that ice cream shop. They are nice people, yes. But Frances is beneath you."

No hurt she had ever felt had hurt her more than this moment, these words. She knew where the iciness came from. In the back of her father's store, where he made the ice cream and bottled the milk, Frances felt a cold that was always there. This was a different cold and it chilled her; it had no explanation for it behind it.

"He's mine now!" Frances burst into the dining room. Frances' face was drawn up and red with pain and tears. "He's mine! I married him! He's not yours any more, Mother Cassity. So keep your hands off him, Mother Cassity. Keep your hands off!"

Frances fled up the stairs.

Five minutes later Leonard was in their bedroom, where Frances' face lay buried in a pillow.

"Frances," he said, "Frances, she did not mean it. Frances, she just told me that. Let her come and apologize to you."

"No."

"Frances."

"No."

"Frances, will you?"

"No. And I will tell you what, Leonard Cassity. I hate her and from this moment I am going to treat her exactly as she treats me. And that's a promise from Frances Smith, from Frances Smith Cassity, and I will tell you what. Frances Smith Cassity keeps her promises."

On the return, a feeling of dark, unfathomable somberness that nothing anyone could say would lift filled the cab of the truck Frances, with eyes red, sat between Leonard and her father her head resting on Leonard's shoulder. She seemed to see nothing.

Leonard had nothing to say. From time to time Mister Smith stole a glance but he had to let the situation lie.

"We have to go back through Monroeville." Mister Smith finally said. "I need sodium hydroxide and the Red Barn Creamery is going to lend me some."

"What is it?" asked Leonard, happy to see any new subject come along.

"Caustic. Helps to sterilize the bottles. We have never, to my knowledge, ever caused a health problem with our product."

They loaded the caustic at the Monroeville dairy and the manager was happy to see Mister Smith and unlock on Sunday. "The son-in-law," he said with a smile and reached for Leonard's hand.

Mister Smith also asked for some milk bottles and the manager helped to load twelve dozen in cases, filling out the back of the truck. The atmosphere seemed slightly better as they turned onto the road to Grove Hill.

"Alabama River. The steam of life," said Mister Smith as they topped the final hill that took them down to the bridge.

A half-mile down lay the river. Mister Smith's loaded truck took on speed.

"Daddy, can you go slower?" asked Frances. Mister Smith pushed the brakes but they did not seem to help much. "Old brakes," he said.

Mister Smith braked again. The dairy truck had begun to vibrate. "Hot, I guess. Fading out. The brake shoes are expanded."

"Slow it, Daddy!"

"It won't slow." He stomped again on useless brakes.

Frances could see that the speedometer needle touched fifty now. Then fifty-five. The needle edged toward sixty.

"Daddy, please help," said Frances as Mister Smith grasped the now vibrating steering wheel. To Leonard, Mister Smith could plainly not control this truck. There would be a disaster. A quarter-mile above the bridge now. Frances saw seventy on the needle.

The dairy truck veered from side to side, crossing both lanes of the highway at seventy miles an hour. The front wheels had gone into a crazy wobble that threw the passengers from side to side. Leonard thought the wheels would tear themselves off the frame. *That would be good,* he thought. As the front wheels touched each shoulder Mister Smith yanked the crazy truck back to the center of the road with all his strength.

Leonard heard a bang and saw the right front tire fly, off spewing scraps of rubber along the road. The metal rim brought a shower of sparks from the pavement. Leonard saw the bridge. He took Frances into his arms then pulled her against his chest then hid her face between his shoulders.

"God, Frances, I'm sorry," were the last words Mister Smith ever spoke.

The cargo in the rear continued to move at seventy miles an hour as the abutment brought the truck to a dead stop. The load destroyed the rear of the cabin and the machine in back came through and crushed Mister Smith against the steering wheel. Mister Smith's face was turned toward Frances and his lifeless eyes looked at her quizzically.

Because they were young they did not die. Their bodies hurt.

Almost all parts of them would turn blue.

Frances and Leonard stood on the road alongside the wreck.

Frances, who had cried all weekend, did not cry.

"Leonard," she said in a level voice, "I wish Fergie was here."

TWO

Wɪʟʟɪᴀᴍ Hᴀʀᴏʟᴅ ᴅᴇᴄɪᴅᴇᴅ ᴛᴏ ʀɪꜱᴋ writing the letter.

He rose from his desk, buttoned his vest and reached into the bottom drawer. He straightened his four-in-hand using the small mirror he kept in the drawer. When he did not have a customer to see, he hung his suit coat on a peg behind the office door. The coat had never become wrinkled since the day he bought it from the best haberdasher in Tuscaloosa. Now he inspected the shoulders for flecks, put on the coat and stepped into the lobby.

"Miss Hearn," he said.

Miss Hearn sat outside Mr. Harold's office door. Everyone entering the bank could see that the person in the office behind Miss Hearn, simply by virtue of having a Miss Hearn, must be important.

Miss Hearn did not look up. She had a pencil clamped in her teeth and said "Yes, sir," without removing the pencil. Miss Hearn was petite, pretty; and Miss Hearn's hair was never out of place. Miss Hearn typed the letters and answered the phone, saying in a friendly Southern voice "State Bank of Clarke."

William Harold the Third had hired her last summer, a day after she graduated from Mississippi State College for Women at Columbus. Miss Hearn's father owned the telephone exchange, and Mister Harold believed Miss Hearn was a prize catch for the bank, keeping her out of the hands of any other bank in Thomasville, although Thomasville did not have any other banks, but might, some day. Caution ruled the life of William Harold the Third. Miss Hearn added to the reputation of the bank.

She removed the pencil she used to underline key thoughts from the small book of daily inspirations in her hand.

"Miss Hearn, get me the key to the Gordon property, will you?" Mr. Harold said. The future lay in chain stores, and in Thomasville the future was now. William Harold the Third had just made that decision. He had read the big daily papers. Everyone at the Deke house read the papers.

"And get me the usual report also, please."

It was a custom William Harold the Third had acquired from his great-uncle, Francis X. Harold, who founded the State Bank of Clarke using the last of the cotton money. Francis X., at age 94, remained the sole stockholder. Once a week, on Mondays at ten, William Harold the Third drove out to Francis X.'s white-columned home to learn how to run the bank.

Francis X. always handed notes to William Harold the Third, written in a creaky pencil scrawl on the backs of envelopes and so forth. The notes said things like "be careful about lending money to so-and-so. He was a payment late in 1911," and "Do not pay interest on money until the day after receipt as it is impossible to employ the money on the day received."

At the end of every session Francis X. would stand and hold out a weak and bony hand and say, "You're a good boy, Bill." No one ever called him "Bill" except Francis X. He detested being called "Bill."

In his active days, any time Francis X. left the bank for the streets of Thomasville he had carried in his pocket a slip of paper which told him that day's bank balances for the customers he was most likely to encounter. A banker's duty was to know as much about the customers—for the benefit of the stockholders—as possible. Even if the stockholders were just him. The balance determined the degree of cordiality with which he would greet the customer, who had all been completely unaware of how Francis X. Harold carried out his role in the town as its principal banker.

William Harold the Third carried on the tradition.

Miss Hearn went to the ledgers and copied down some numbers. "Are you just going to the Gordon property?" she asked. .

"Yes."

"I think these will do." There were about four numbers.

"Thank you," said Mister Harold.

He brushed a fleck off his coat then headed outdoors.

The Gordons had sold general merchandise—a solid enterprise—but they were not good business people, and they'd struggled. Perhaps they could have stayed in business, but they had never recovered from the loss of their son in France. The Gordons believed he had been clubbed to death by German soldiers; stories of German clubbings ran commonly in the press. It was an unspoken thought between them, and even without words it added to the sadness they felt together. But everything made them sadder. Anything about the war. Mister Gordon would come to the front of the store with eyes red from tears. Finally customers decided it was just better not to shop there.

William Harold the Third remembered the auction. His great-uncle made him go—to attend to the bank's interest—and he'd bought the property back in for the amount of the mortgage.

The former Gordon Mercantile sat at the end of the block on the opposite side of the street from the bank. It was a tidy two-story red brick building with a row of show windows recessed behind an arched arcade. Customers could browse the windows in the shade. Large double doors stood at the corner behind the arches.

Debris had accumulated in the arcade and the windows were dirty. Tomorrow William Harold the Third would have Jerome, the bank's porter and handyman, go over there with brooms and buckets and sponges.

The door took his attention.

If I had thought to bring a ruler or a yardstick or something.

Not having any, he spread his arms across the doors and estimated. *I am nearly six feet, and there is a little more than six feet of space here. About enough for a small one.*

He let himself in.

Inside he found much more dust than he expected. Everything glass, from the windows to the cases, was clouded over, with dust and he made several squiggly lines. Tomorrow he would have Miss Hearn locate two colored women to clean. She knew how to locate that kind of help. He studied the cash register. He pushed the two dollar key and the drawer opened with a *ching!* It still worked. *A sales point*, he thought.

The mercantile's staircase made a creaky sound, as if the building was sighing at its circumstances. All four window shades had been torn by someone who obviously hadn't known that window shades will not roll. William Harold the Third tried one. "Well, *that* one rolls," he remarked grimly, as he watched it wrap around its roller. He dragged a toe across the floor. Deep dust. *Stuff you can't even mop up*, he thought. *Still leaves a powder*. He scowled at the remnants of a small bird's carcass. How could something have gotten inside with a bird to devour? He looked at scattered papers, bills, a last year's calendar, a store flyer, a Birmingham newspaper that shouted in four inch letters ARMISTICE!

He had known the Gordon son slightly because they were not much apart in age but William Harold the Third did not expect him to enroll at the University of Alabama. He had not and William Harold the Third had, and had become a member of the Delta Kappa Epsilon fraternity. The Gordon son had gone to war. .

After twenty minutes he locked up the store; convinced that he was right about its future. On his walk back to the bank he stopped in Miss Eloise McCord's little flower shop. There was always a wedding or a funeral in Thomasville, enough to make for a small deposit from Miss Eloise. But she must also have recently clipped the interest coupon from the late Mister McCord's Chicago, Burlington and Quincy bonds and so he ordered some flowers for the lobby.

After William returned to the office he hung the coat, unbuttoned his vest and asked Miss Hearn to bring him a pencil and one of her steno pads.

THE CLARKE COUNTY DEMOCRATS

STATE BANK OF CLARKE

SERVING WEST ALABAMA

P.O. BOX 9 TEL 44 THOMASVILLE, ALABAMA   OFFICE IN GROVE HILL

February 2, 1920

Mister Aaron Silverstein, President
George Washington's All-American Stores
13th Floor
Einhorn Building
Meridian Mississippi

Dear Mister Silverstein:

Let me introduce myself as vice president and chief accountant of
the State Bank of Clarke .("Serving West Alabama")

Mister Silverstein, we wish to make a solid business proposition
to you. We are aware, as you are well aware, that the old General
Store method of merchandising is outmoded and obsolete1 and that
you are a pioneer! Your slogan "Remember the Maine? No! Forget the
Maine! Remember our Prices!" says it all!

You are fast-proving that the chain store is a great boon to a
community and now we offer the opportunity to come to thriving
Thomasville.

This bank has acquired by way of foreclosure one of the choicest
retail locations in this city. We would like to discuss with you
the possibility of a George Washington's All American here.

To succeed, the department store must offer its goods in artistic
surroundings and this location has that potential. The key, as
you know, is "display and sell" and "what is displayed, sells" and
this location is equipped with glass display cases!

I propose nothing less than success! Families living with average
incomes achieve success because they show concern how they spend
their money. They know wise spending builds character and the
George Washington All American chain is synonymous with character.

My hero the great economist Thomas N. Carver says "the nations
which take their leisure in the form of frequent holidays,
graceful consumption and elegant leisure have long since fallen
behind the process of civilization". And I can assure you this
does not describe the hard-working wise citizens of Thomasville!

Additional points: the community can furnish you excellent
salesladies and seamstresses. Women of high character who attend
church and will attract through your doors their many friends.

```
As if these attractions are not enough let me make this
unbelievable offer. This bank will consider installing at its own
expense a revolving door! Customers will come from miles away to
see this unique portal and once having entered without hindrance
will buy!

Mister Silverstein, I serve in the additional capacity of business
manager for our local baseball team and I must visit Meridian soon
to "talk a little baseball" with other managers. I would consider
it an honor to speak to you personally then.

And hoorah for the red, white and blue, Mister Silverstein. Hoorah
for the red, white and blue!

Yours truly,

William Harold III
Vice President and Chief Accountant
```

Miss Hearn edited the letter, toning down extravagances and removing some of the exclamation points. She added "III" to William Harold's signature, saying it added authority, and she personally walked the letter to the mailbox.

○ ○ ○

From nowhere near the kind of money he needed by opening game Aaron Silverstein had put together in cash around $70,000. He placed all of it on the Cincinnati Red Stockings to win the 1919 World Series, which they did.

The lawyer in Aaron Silverstein, however, told the gambler in Aaron Silverstein that the lid was going to come off the scandal and it would be good for such a small time player to escape notice.

Aaron Silverstein had very respectable relatives in Meridian and it was a good place to hide from the heat. The Sears Roebuck connection, of course, would never come to light, and so Aaron Silverstein decided he would set up a chain of outlets for pilfered Sears's merchandise.

At age 42, hiding out in Meridian he used the Black Sox winnings to establish a chain of department stores in smaller cities around the South. Jews in retailing often used Gentile or patriotic names for their businesses, always conscious of anti-Semitism. Who, Aaron Silverstein thought, could be more patriotic than George Washington?

George Washington's All American stores advertised merchandise "as good as Sears Roebuck at half the Sears Roebuck price." It was a claim he could definitely make because it was Sears Roebuck's merchandise that he was selling, stolen in Chicago from the gigantic Sears Roebuck warehouses. And Sears Roebuck never had in its warehouses what Sears' books said it had.

Miss Hearn presented the typed letter. "Mister Harold, don't you think Thomasville is a little bit, well…."

"Yes?"

"Well….tired?"

"Tired?"

"Well, there's not much here…."

"Miss Hearn. I have researched this. It is in all the papers. It is time to think ahead. See into the future, Miss Hearn. See into the future."

"I mean it's sort of timbered out."

"No. And it never will be. We must not think that way. What we need is boosting. Not knocking. That is one reason why I made myself available as business manager of the Clarke County Democrats. That team boosts the city. And when the season opens it would be very nice to see you in the stands rooting, Miss Hearn. It is what we need. I will not hear any more of that. That is all. Thank you, Miss Hearn."

Looking forward to her graduation the next June, Miss Hearn presented her resume' to Mister Harold between Christmas and New Year of 1918. For his part, Mister Harold knew it was time to make a payment to the Modern Woman. She sat erect across from his desk in a starched blouse, her hands properly in her lap.

"Let's me see," he said.

Mister Harold read "major, English Literature, B.A. President, senior and junior class. Poet, sophomore and freshman class. Equal Suffrage League. Good, good."

"But a non-Prohibition suffragist."

"Not the anti-Saloon kind?"

"….Mister Harold…a little toddy now and then?"

"And of course the Amendment."

"When passed I will obey it."

"Do not mention it to people very much."

"Naturally."

He resumed reading.

"Also, Story Tellers' League. Dramatic Club. Classical Club. Fire Chief. *Fire chief?*"

Miss Hearn gave a slight shrug.

"*And mistress of herself, though China fall'?*"

"It's Pope."

"Electives, in commercial law, bookkeeping and 'household accounting'. What is 'household accounting'?"

"That's double-entry bookkeeping, check book management and understanding commercial paper."

Miss Hearn appeared to Mister Harold to meet the requirements for a Modern Woman, however she would need to keep quiet on the non-Prohibition part, and so she came to work the day after she graduated,

William Harold the Third sent the letter out on a Monday. A week and a half later he had a reply. Mister Silverstein would like to hear more about Thomasville. He suggested a date two weeks ahead at his office in Meridian. Please confirm by return mail.

◯ ◯ ◯

Two weeks later William Harold the Third tapped at the door marked George Washington Stores on the thirteenth floor of the Einhorn Building in Meridian, Mississippi.

The principal offices seemed to consist of nothing but one room.

The man who answered the door had dark eyes and salt and pepper black hair. The dark eyes gave William Harold the Third a look from head to toe.

"Come in, Bill," he said.

Aaron Silverstein led William Harold the Third to a chair next to a desk which were the only furnishings in the room. There was a portrait of George Washington over the desk.

"Should I call you Bill?" he asked.

"It's William mostly," he responded.

"William," replied Silverstein in a confirming kind of a tone. "Then tell me about Thomasville, Alabama," and for twenty minutes William Harold the Third described the town. Aaron Silverstein asked why the retail store had failed and he explained that the owners had seemingly just lost interest in life.

Aaron Silverstein tilted back his chair and watched the ceiling for a few moments. "I'd like to visit your city," he said finally. Then he added "so you're here to talk to some baseball people?"

"I want to arrange some games if I can. We can travel now. We have recently acquired a nice bus. Of course I'd like to be invited to the big Casey Jones series but that won't be easy. They can get anyone they want."

"'Casey Jones'? I'm pretty new here."

"Big weekend series. The host is the M&O Railroad's Firebox Stokers. The Stokers are a team that comes from up and down the whole line. But if I can get us one game this year they can see how good we are. And maybe get us in line for a year from now."

Silverstein shrugged. "Well, good luck with it. Perhaps I'll see your team play one of these days. I've been around the game since I was young. Meantime, we have to get our visit out of the way. Two weeks from today?"

Of course he could never be a Deke, William Harold the Third thought as he left. *Jewish.* And the flecks he noticed in the hair.

Dandruff.

Some psoriasis; hard to cure. At the Deke house he covered his head with coal tar shampoo every other night. Jews are known not to be clean. But there's the baseball. Showed interest there. So if it's baseball in common, let it be baseball.

○ ○ ○

The stairs made that noise again and that prepared Miss Hearn.

She stood at the top of the steps hands on hips, dressed today in the navy gymnasium suit she put away at graduation from Mississippi State College for Women. Her brow was moist. She did not wait for Mister Harold to speak.

"What are you doing here, Mister Harold? If you're here, pick up a mop." She poofed a lock off the brow. "Do you have the bunting?"

Miss Hearn's idea was that if the store was to be a George Washington's All American store, the building should be decked out in red, white and blue for the visit of the president of the George Washington stores.

"I, uh…."

"Mister Harold…."

"I'll go see."

Mister Harold had placed the order through Miss Eloise at the flower shop who telegraphed the order to Montgomery through Doctor Pearlington and the drugstore and Western Union office.

Main Street Thomasville therefore knew everything about the coming visit of the George Washington stores and it had sprung to life.

William Harold the Third had informed his great-uncle Francis X Harold of the prospect, who said "You're a good boy, Bill," but that was all he said.

William Harold the Third retreated and as he exited the store he bumped into Miss Eloise who struggled with a large box. "Mister Harold, you are a genius," Miss Eloise said. "No, no," Mister Harold said back, in a very modest tone.

So, he reascended the stairs with the box. "The bunting is here," he said to Miss Hearn who had heard him coming again. She poofed a lock of hair off her moist forehead and said "good" very curtly.

Two black cleaning women had taken an interest in Miss Hearn and Mister Harold.

"What are you looking at?" Miss Hearn turned and demanded. "*Work.*"

The following morning Miss Hearn was at her desk with not a hair out of place.

The phone jangled and Miss Hearn answered "State Bank of Clarke" in a sweet voice.

"No, Mister Silverstein arrives tomorrow," she said to the caller. No, Mister Harold will definitely want you to meet him. Mister Harold knows he needs insurance. No, Mister Harrigan. Yes, I will tell him. Thank you.

"That was Mister Harrigan," said Miss Hearn," telling Mister Harold as he came from his office to learn who was calling. "Oh," said Mister Harold and returned to his office.

THREE

"Say, Leonard." Cobb came walking over.

If Cobb ever came to work in clean clothes Leonard might like him better. Frances packed Leonard a lunch. Cobb never brought anything for lunch.

Cobb ran the big circular saw. The saw ripped giant pine logs into lumber. Sawdust covered him over. That was what he looked like by lunchtime. By the end of a day the work made him into a kind of statue of piney sawdust.

"Havin' my lunch, Cobb."

"Yep." Cobb drawled it out then sat down.

At the noon whistle Leonard had gone to a stack of green two-by-fours and turned his lunch pail upside down.

"Say, Leonard, you want to make some money?"

Leonard took the cornbread out of the cloth napkin Frances always packed.

Cobb looked at Leonard's cornbread then opened his legs and spat tobacco juice at the ground. "Cornbread," he said. Leonard broke it in two.

"You can make a little if you know how to play some ball."

"What kind of ball?"

"Baseball. What other kind is there?"

"Golf ball, Cobb. Somebody could play golf ball." Cobb often did not let Leonard eat his lunch alone. The big circular blade, almost as tall as Leonard tore through logs with a screaming vengeance and Leonard wanted the half hour to get the scream out of his ears. He also wanted the time to think about the future.

"You mean with one of them little sticks? Sheee-it."

"Want to eat, Cobb."

"Suit yourself. You told me you played. There's three to four dollars a Sunday."

"How much?"

"Could be as much as five. You said you was a good player when you was young."

Cobb spat again. Sometimes the tobacco juice did not reach the ground. Sometimes it landed in the crotch of his overalls.

"Say, Leonard?"

"Umnnn."

"How'd you get this job? Bein' from Mobile. Just driftin'?"

"They told my daddy out where he's building the paper mill. Ground up job. Here, take half my peanut butter cookie."

"Me? I didn't have no daddy."

"Your daddy didn't have no kid."

"He had me."

"You was born just like you are."

"A young married man like you needs money."

"I get a paycheck."

"I got paid five dollars one time. Collected a hit."

"A hit ain't nothin'."

"Won a game. Popped it straight into center field." Cobb straightened his arm in the direction of center field. "Would have been six dollars but I got thrown out. I stopped running. Mister Harrigan said I lost interest in the game between first and second. Truly, though, it wasn't my fault.

The outfielder should have thrown it to third. I just wanted to see what would happen."

"What happened?"

"He threw the ball to the first baseman who was standing next to me watching, too."

"You want me to play on a team like that?"

"This Mister Harrigan, he's serious business." The juice landed in Cobb's crotch, which was already brown. Leonard had never seen him in clean overalls. "Bought us a bus. His money. Clarke County Democrats. What'd you play?"

"Pitched some."

"Twirler, huh? Got a curve?"

"Don't bother with them. Too fast for people."

"I bet we got people would knock you out of the park. I said to Mister Harrigan 'At the sawmill is a young man who told me once he was a baseball player.' 'Bring him over,' Mister Harrigan said."

"I didn't come here to play ball," Leonard said impatiently.. "Don't anybody play ball anymore when they're married."

"Your wife might like the money. My old lady lets me in her bed if I give her the money. You didn't know I had a old lady. She's common law."

"What's common law?"

"No preacher."

"Cobb, I'll just come down there and strike out your whole team then go home."

"You couldn't strike out them two Indians."

"Indians can't hit."

"You ever seen an Indian hit?"

"No. I ain't. But I know."

"Indians dream. And what's more they can jump up in the air and just hang there. Now don't tell me I haven't seen that because I have. And I don't know if they can both do it but one can."

"White men hit. Not Indians. Who's Mister Harrigan?"

"He's a big insurance man in town. He put the team together to boost up the town. I'll tell you who'd like to see you strike out the Indians."

"Who?"

"Buckles would. He had a ancestor scalped by Indians."

O O O

"Sunday is church day, Leonard," Frances said. "I ain't never missed church."

"Frances, I won eleven games in high school. Lost one. And how would it be if I made five or six dollars on a Sunday? I can see lots of things coming into this house with that money. Wouldn't be but a couple of months this summer. Jesus don't give a hoot about baseball."

"He gives a hoot about you."

"Here's why Jesus don't give a hoot about baseball. You want to know?"

"Leonard, I know you want the money for us, but….Well, why?"

"Jesus don't give a hoot because baseball just ain't got no reason to be."

"Ain't?"

"Baseball ain't got no reason to be there. It's just a sport. It don't do nothing for you. You just do it. So Jesus don't give a hoot about something ain't got no reason to be."

"I don't know, Leonard. You're not supposed to get along without Jesus. If Jesus wants you in church, you can't let baseball get in the way. I wish I was you, Leonard. Am I smart enough for you? Do I just don't understand why you can play and Jesus don't give a hoot about it? If it don't matter that you play, don't play and come to church."

"I'm only gonna play it for the money. Not because I like the sport. Not because I'm good at it. That's kid stuff.

"Frances, I want to try it. If I don't have what it takes I'll just forget about it. I ain't a loser. You'll find out I ain't a loser. Don't never come home whipped."

"You'll still have it, Leonard. So don't say that. But besides, we were married in the sight of God."

"And ain't you never seen Jesus at the baseball park?"

"He don't go there on Sunday or any day."

"You don't know. He would go if he liked the team. Without me he don't give a hoot about the Clarke County Democrats.

"Try for it, Leonard. I'm a wife and a wife follows her husband. Maybe it's God's way. God will speak to me or you about this. If God speaks to you about playing baseball will you listen to what he tells you?"

Leonard said nothing through supper. Jesus don't give a hoot about baseball. Some things were just too important to talk about. Some things were not important enough to talk about.

○ ○ ○

Leonard had a very bad dream. He was Cobb. He had never left the sawmill. A young man who looked like him sat next to him at the noon whistle. "What's your name?" he asked. "Leonard Cassity, Junior," said the boy.

Leonard woke up sweating. Frances was asleep. Sometimes she whimpered in her sleep but he never said anything about it. It was what she had been through. She could be having bad dreams, too. He got up and went to the kitchen and picked up last night's dish towel. He walked outside and put his head under the pump and doused his head and shoulders with cold water.

He walked to the privy and sat down.

He strained. Strained to go. Strained to hear God. Nothing either way.

"Leonard?" a voice whispered. "Oh, God!" Leonard leaped off the seat.

"Leonard, are you all right?" Frances whispered again.

"I'm all right. I just felt a kind of a twinge."

Frances came in and plopped down next to Leonard.

"I don't know why they make these things with two holes. Me and Fergie used to do this together," she giggled. In a little while they went back to the house. Unless Frances was God he would go down to join the Clarke County Democrats.

FOUR

At Meridian, Aaron Silverstein read the letter and prepared a reply. Only one paragraph actually interested him. The paragraph about baseball.

When Aaron Silverstein was sixteen years old his father sent him from Chicago to New York to live with an uncle and be apprenticed in the garment business. Instead, the uncle, so Aaron's embittered father later said, turned Aaron into a "hoodlum" who only cared about gambling. "Turn aside from this, Aaron," his father pleaded. His father proposed the University of Chicago Law School. Aaron graduated with the class of 1907. A smart lawyer, but with nothing genius about him. Aaron took more seriously the education he had gotten as a young lowlife and troublemaker from the pool halls and the streets of the Lower East Side of New York. At Yom Kippur a year after his graduation when he had never taken a case his father disowned him. "Aaron the sham. Aaron the imposter," he said and made a raspberry with his tongue.

The Black Sox scandal brought Aaron to Meridian, a decision his father forced on him days after the *New York World* broke the story that the 1919 World Series had been fixed. Aaron's father read the papers and sought out Aaron. "Is your name going to be in the paper? Never mind.

You will kill your mother with this, you know. Aaron, you have relatives. Honest relatives. Go there. I will fix it up. Say you didn't know." Aaron told his honest relatives just that.

Naturally, Aaron knew all about it, and knew almost before anyone.

Aaron had a good friend whose name was Abe Attell and Abe Attell had much to do with putting in the fix. Attell had a good record as a featherweight boxer, a Jewish boxer called "the Little Hebrew," who put substances on his gloves and did other illegal things. Aaron Silverstein liked to bet on dirty prizefights and so he made friends with the Little Hebrew. He won money on the Little Hebrew's fights.

Attell became more famous as the go-between for Arnold Rothstein, the professional gambler who put up $100,000 to pay off to the eight White Socks players who became known as the Black Sox. Rothstein was said to have bet $270,000 on Cincinnati to win the series. Anytime Attell had something to report to Rothstein, however, he first told his good friend Aaron Rothstein about it.

A week before the Series began Attell told Silverstein "Cicotte has come on board." Eddie Cicotte was the pitcher who would start the first game for the White Sox and he would be a key figure if the Series was going to be fixed. Aaron Silverstein began to gather up his money.

Aaron Silverstein had some money but not much. He had his winnings from prizefighting, but those totaled only in the low thousands and he wanted a lot more. He thought that he might steal his uncle Abe's new car and sell it to the bootleggers then steal it or buy it back, but that would only net him a few hundred and not nearly enough. Finally he came up with the great scheme that would supply him with the money he wanted.

Aaron Silverstein's apprenticeship in the garment industry in New York paid off. About garments, he may have learned a little. About men he had learned a lot. And many men from the Little Sicily neighborhood had found work in the Sears Roebuck warehouses. Sears had grown so large it distributed mail order catalogues in the millions.

In New York Aaron Silverstein had learned to speak a few words of Italian and to loll in the coffee houses over Italian coffee, talking banalities, always on the lookout for a chance. The Italian underworld passed through Italian coffee houses, it was accepted as everyday, and it did not take Aaron

Silverstein very long in the Italian neighborhoods to find a few Sears warehouse workers. He bought the coffee. He talked. He outlined the idea, first as a suggestion, and then he listened as the warehousemen explained how it could be done. They liked to talk. Aaron Silverstein convinced them they could put together a pilferage racket on grand scale and that he could help. The warehousemen went back and talked it over with their foreman. The foreman talked to his manager who contributed his own ideas about pilferage. Sears had pitifully poor inventory practices.

In the dead of night Sears merchandise began to move out warehouse doors and onto Aaron Silverstein's trucks. The trucks delivered whole racks of apparel from the warehouses to the empty building Aaron Rothstein rented. Aaron Silverstein spent days and nights ripping the Sears Roebuck labels out of clothes. He chainsmoked and did not sleep.

He had only days now. But he spent those days living the life of a peddler, driving a truck from town to town all the way from Milwaukee on the Wisconsin side to Gary on the Indiana side, talking to merchants, enticing them to the street where he opened wide the doors, displaying racks of clothing "every bit as good as Sears Roebuck in quality" and selling it for pennies on the dollar. All for cash.

On the day Aaron Silverstein was to arrive, Mister and Mrs. Gordon prepared early to watch the event. Thornton Gordon had wrapped his arms around his wife and held back his tears. She said "can you take me to that place where you go, Thornton?' and there wasn't anything else he could do.

Since the foreclosure Miss Eloise McCord became a visitor to Mister and Mrs. Gordon at their home. Usually she brought with her a box of tea, or some candy or crackers she had ordered for the gift shop side of her shop. She liked Mrs. Gordon and when the Gordons had their business she dropped into the store almost every day to share the small talk of Main Street. Mrs. Gordon described the latest letter from Robert in France. The letters never said anything about action, never said anything despairing,

Robert had seemingly gone over to France to have a picnic. And then there was the letter from the War Department.

Mrs. Gordon wasted. She lost weight and became gray faced. At times she could not make herself come out front to greet a customer. Mister Gordon took on the whole burden of the store, but he was very straight-laced and no good at small talk and had no sense whatever for what a customer wanted, even if the customer did not say it for himself.

On the day he had to go to the bank and inform Mister Harold that he could not make the payment, he delayed. He wandered about Main Street for two hours, peering into shop windows, rehearsing his statement.

Mister Harold sympathized, he listened patiently. And when he went out for his weekly meeting with Francis X. Harold he did not mention it. He felt guilty. He thought the situation would be better by next month. The Gordons' financial situation got no better.

Mister Harold had to tell the whole story now. Two payments had been missed; all Francis X. Harold said was "how many payments?" When William Harold the Third departed Francis X. stood and said "you're a good boy, Bill," and William Harold the Third knew the whole burden would fall on him. On the third missed payment he made no effort to hide his dejection from his great-uncle. His great-uncle simply said "you'll have to call in the loan". As he left, he heard Francis X. Harold say in a soft voice "you're a good boy, Bill".

And now Mister and Mrs. Gordon did not show their faces in town. They went to church once and Mrs. Gordon came home and wept quietly all afternoon. If Mister Gordon entered the room she straightened herself and pretended to be mending something. But the Gordons buried themselves behind their curtains in their shame and humiliation. And in their grief.

Miss Eloise began to make her visits but she only answered questions if asked, and she never brought anything up other than whatever was cheerful. The George Washington's All-American event was different, however, since it involved their old store. Eloise McCord took a deep breath and said a silent prayer. She told them everything she knew.

In the middle of the narrative Mrs. Gordon interrupted. "Eloise?" she asked. There was what Eloise had hoped for, a glimmer. "What's that, dear?" she said.

"Do you suppose they…."

"What, dear?"

"Oh, no, nothing. Never mind."

"I don't know," said Eloise, smiling. "But I will do my best. Yes, I will do my best."

"And Eloise…."

"Yes, dear?"

"If you know any families who need any mending…."

"You have my word."

The Gordons decided they wanted to see the upcoming event, the event that would alter the fate of their old store. Mister Gordon described for Mrs. Gordon a place behind some shrubs. They would watch from there.

Mister Gordon began to observe the preparations. He observed from nowhere near Main Street but from a spot surrounded by shrubs about two hundred feet away. He could see just enough. He saw someone, he did not know who, remove the shades from the upstairs windows of the old store. Every morning that young woman from the bank marched from store to store. Even from the distance he could hear her heels on the sidewalks.

For Miss Hearn her Main Street campaign did not differ from her campaigns for Junior or senior class president. Or for class poet. Gentle persuasion. But dominance. No political message now, just "clean it up, paint it up, fix it up. This new store will help *you.*" And the store would help Miss Hearn.

Once a year Miss Hearn's father took them all to Memphis to shop. Now, she realized, in the foreseeable future, she would be able to go shopping at home in Thomasville.

The chain store would offer styles! Not just one style. Sizes! Not just a few sizes and not your size, just not in anything you'd want. Shoes! Away with button hooks. Pretty towels, or sheets. Perfumes and sachets and toilet water. Jasmine! Heavenly jasmine! Powder puffs. If Miss Hearn had to alter the fate of Thomasville could shop for powder puffs, she would do it.

Thus, Mister Gordon became transfixed by the sight of her. Without even knowing her mission, he became addicted to it. And from behind his shrub he urged her on. Head erect, backbone straight, sometimes bringing the shop owner outside his door to point something or another out, clearly remonstrative, Miss Hearn changed Main Street.

The day arrived. The second Saturday in April. A warm morning after a pleasant night.

The only crowd ever larger had been the Armistice on November 11, 1918, when people rushed into the streets banging broomsticks and mop handles on washtubs. The red, white and blue bunting which Miss Eloise McCord ordered and Miss Hearn had hung fluttered across the building front in the soft breeze.

Miss Hearn arrived at the front door of the Gordon Building one hour ahead of the scheduled arrival of Aaron Silverstein and arranged the welcoming dignitaries in their places.

She placed the mayor to make the first handshake, followed by Win Harrigan the chairman of the Chamber of Commerce booster committee; William Harold the Third stood next to Mister Harrigan; Mister Shaw, principal at the Institute in position to cue the band and nearby, herself as the general assistant. She stole a glance toward the two shadows behind the shrubs two hundred feet from the door.

Thirty minutes late a Ford appeared at the end of Main Street. Two blocks down Edgar Thompson, owner of Thompson's Hardware, stepped into the street and pumped a lantern up and down. It was a signal for people to begin to appear and to walk the streets, coming and going into stores. Miss Hearn had dispatched Edgar simply to wave an arm when the car came into sight. Thompson took the lantern off the shelf, adding it as his own idea even though the sun shone on a cloudless morning.

Literally Edgar Thompson raised the curtain on an opera, an opera Miss Hearn had created.

At the bandstand, Fingers the best musician in Thomasville, readied a snare drum. A cornet and a trombone made up the rest of the band. Fingers and Miss Hearn had gone over the music. First a drumroll, leading to a march; next a short piece of ragtime, finally something patriotic as the welcoming party entered the store.

Aaron Silverstein stepped from the car and his dark eyes roamed across the scene. A black forelock fell over an eyebrow and he brushed it back.

Aaron Silverstein was not who Miss Hearn expected. In her mind she had created Aaron Silverstein as someone godlike, heaven sent, to descend from his Ford but to recognize immediately that all this as her work, to see her in that instant as a worthy peer. That was hard to expect from a man who approached the committee with a careless, pigeon-toed shamble, who wore no jacket, no four-in-hand, only an open collar, herringbone trousers in a wide black and silver zigzag and belt with a gigantic silver buckle. "Is this Thomasville, Alabama?" he asked.

FIVE

WHILE TWO MEN OUT AT the bandstand who William Harold the Third recognized as the infielders, *those Indians*, beat on what looked like tom-toms, and Fingers executed a fanfare on the cornet, the party entered the store. They passed down aisles of gleaming glass cases. At the cash register William Harold the Third pressed the two-dollar key and the register went "*ching.*" He knelt before the safe and twirled the dial. Then he opened the safe. He closed the door, twirled the knob and opened the safe again. "Secure as a bank," he said. "Almost as secure," he corrected himself.

The mayor said "excuse me", shook hands and left. All the time, Aaron Silverstein gave polite attention, but no one knew what he thought. After about fifteen minutes, including the look upstairs, he said "efficient layout." Everyone smiled.

The party now stood at the rear of the store looking toward the aisles and the display windows. William Harold the Third said "Miss Hearn, will you show Mister Silverstein the fitting room arrangement, I should go and dismiss the band."

"My pleasure, sir," said Miss Hearn.

Miss Hearn pulled back a curtain. "As you can see, sir, complete privacy for the patron. Mirrors. A work area with ironing boards. Two Singer machines."

"So I see."

"I will thread one."

"Yes."

"The professional seamstress does this smoothly, but this goes in here." She took an end of thread. "They taught us this in dressmaking."

"I believe it goes in there." Aaron Silverstein pointed.

"Here?'

"Yes, here. May I help?"

Miss Hearn stepped aside.

"I worked in the garment industry before law school. It's working now," said Aaron Silverstein.

"Yes, thank you. It works perfectly."

"Yes, it does," Aaron Silverstein agreed.

"Mister Silverstein," said Miss Hearn, "may I speak frankly to you?"

"Please do."

"Mister Silverstein, I applaud the George Washington's All-American stores. They are a celebration of American life. Mister Silverstein, I am liberal arts major and I find in them a statement of our cultural values here in America. And your claim to 'merchandise comparable to Sears Roebuck at half the price' is conclusive proof of the dominance of the American spirit. And may I be frank?"

"Why shouldn't you be?"

"God has designated you. God has designated you as the embodiment of the American spirit as what America is all about."

"I don't think I would say that."

"And Mister Silverstein, I appeal to your Christian duty to open a store in Thomasville."

"I am not a Christian."

"Your whatever you are."

"I am a Jew."

"And that does not mean you do not have a Christian duty."

"My duty as a Jew."

"Mister Silverstein, I am not rigid. Mister Silverstein, I can vote. Or will be able to when I am twenty-one, which I will be. And I will vote for the Republican who I think will be Mister Harding and the Return to Normalcy."

"I am a Democrat."

"Bully."

"I will vote for the Democrat."

"Bully, bully."

○ ○ ○

Back in Meridian Aaron Silverstein came to grips with choices. The claims Mister Harold made about the sales potential in a small town like that were so much boosterism and so much hooey. With that thought he placed the check book back in the drawer.

On the other hand there were those girlish now fading freckles on the nose of that young woman, Miss Hearn. The prim, starched blouse.

Was that what this suffrage movement was all about? This impending amendment to the United States Constitution? About freckles? Blouses? Assertiveness? He had no idea.

Why did he not know how he felt?

He removed the checkbook from the drawer.

You couldn't go back, he said to himself. *Go back to what? It's always a gamble, isn't it? Life's a gamble .But I'm a gambler and gamblers don't ever gamble on just anything .They bet on sure things. So why don't I know how I feel?*

He opened the checkbook.

SIX

Tallahatta Springs, Alabama
June 8, 1920

Dear Mother Cassity

I guess you will be surprised to hear from me but there is something I
have to write and I better get right at it.

I want to tell you that I got saved from all my sins last Tuesday night.
We are having the greatest revival that has ever been here. The Rev.
Harold J. Criswell is running it and me and the people I know are all
going. Leonard has been going too but he ain't been saved and I say it is
because he is playing baseball. I say baseball is a sin because it is played
on Sunday but Leonard says Jesus don't give a hoot about baseball.
Baseball would not be a sin if it was played on any day but Sunday and
there ain't no way he can go to church and still play in the game because
the game starts at noon. I have to say I have some sympathy for
Leonard because they pay Leonard $2.00 for every game because he is

the best pitcher they got. I know the revival has softened his heart and you will be pleased to hear that at least.

Your daughter in law
Frances Cassity

◯ ◯ ◯

The revival began the Saturday before the Democrats' opening game on Sunday against the team from Greensboro, a town about sixty miles north. Leonard had worked hard to make the curve ball break straight down. He had regained some of the cockiness he wore that summer he made all state honorable mention. He planned to win. He planned to make the six dollars.

Reverend Criswell's dusty Ford truck rolled into Thomasville on Friday afternoon. The man on personal, speaking terms with hell, with Satan, parked in front of Ferguson's Feed and Seed as he had been told.

Brother Fred Wolverton at Second Baptist had invited Reverend Criswell to town for a week of revival.

Until a year ago Brother Fred had helped out at First Baptist Thomasville but he believed in Holy Hands and the pastor Reverend Dan Danielson believed in just sitting, no holy hands. Some in the First Baptist congregation called Brother Fred to a new church; now Brother Fred pastored Second Baptist. Frances' friend Fergie whose father owned the feed and seed, attended Second Baptist. Mister Ferguson put up the hundred dollar guarantee to bring the Harold Criswell Ministries to Thomasville. Outside the feed and seed Mister Ferguson also put three dollars into the box marked "for monkey."

Already in June the temperature at noon had reached ninety and the beefy reverend opened the door and laid a large flat foot on the ground. The other followed and outside the truck Reverend Criswell fluffed his shirt to draw in some air and dry the perspiration that made his shirt cling to his chest. He was a man somewhere in his fifties, bald on top, gray at the sides, plain steel-rim glasses; he slammed the door, always ready to wage war with hell.

From the bed of the truck he lifted a large sign with black letters outlined in red: "Revival," it said. Reverend Criswell lowered the tailgate and reached for something which turned out to be an old cigar box. He lifted the lid and placed in the box a one dollar bill. A passerby saw the box, which had a note in pencil on it saying "for monkey" and he too placed a dollar bill in the box.

Reverend Criswell mounted the truck and took up a megaphone.

"And my people, upon whom my name is called," he shouted into the megaphone, "shall make supplication to me and seek out my face, and do penance for their wicked ways then I will hear from heaven and will forgive their sins and will heal their land.

"Second Chronicles, Seven fourteen.

"I call out his name."

A man hurried past and Reverend Criswell aimed the megaphone at the man. "Brother, are you saved?" he asked.

Saturday night after supper they sat on the porch and Frances tried to persuade Leonard to go to the revival with her. Leonard held her hand. "Moon tonight," he said.

"Leonard, will you go to the revival with me?"

"What's he talk about?"

"About everything. Little bit about dancin'."

"You'd look pretty dancin'."

"Leonard, not him, but his brother is a preacher, is got a chimpanzee. He puts the chimpanzee up on the stand where he preaches. Now he brings out a dog and the dog starts barking at the chimpanzee. Now he says if people came down from monkeys and not Adam, the chimpanzee would already be smart enough to stop the dog from barking but he cant. This proves that people came down from Adam and not monkeys, just like the Bible says."

"But what's a chimpanzee?"

"It's a kind of a monkey. Then his brother asks the people to be as devoted to the chimpanzee as they are to God and they can't do it. Because how can a person be devoted to a monkey? And he says he wishes he had his own monkey instead of talking about his brother's but he don't. Leonard, I sit next to Fergie but it ain't the same. I want to sit next to you."

"Frances, ain't nothin' there for me."

"You wouldn't go for me?"

"I'd go if he had a chimpanzee."

"You wouldn't go for me?"

"I'll go."

So Leonard went. "Oh, I hate sin!" cried Reverend Criswell. "But everybody hates sin. *As a general thing!* But sin ain't a general thing! It's a specific thing. You think you got everybody's sin? No! You got your own sin. Now is the time for you confess. Who wants to stand up? Is it booze? Is it lust? Carnal desire? Cards? Have you slid back in your heart? Tell us, brother, and we can forgive just as Jesus forgives. Who will stand up right this minute? We want to forgive you *right now.*"

"Leonard, maybe you ought to stand up and confess you play baseball," Frances whispered.

"Baseball ain't no sin," Leonard whispered back.

"But baseball leads people away from the church," Frances whispered.

"It don't." Leonard was irritated.

"If baseball wasn't bein' played the church would be full because people wouldn't have nothin' else to do."

Leonard sulked while a fat lady stood up and said she thought her husband had carnal desires while he was alive. But Leonard did not get saved and he continued to play baseball and the Holy Ghost did not enter into him.

○ ○ ○

"Jesus don't give a hoot about baseball." Leonard dried another dish.

"You told me that."

"Know what else Jesus don't give a hoot about?"

"What?'

"Jesus don't give a hoot 'bout dancin'. You know what?"

"What?"

"They got a music store in Meridian."

"And?"

"Well, it's got a music box. You know, a talking machine. Victrolas they call them.

"So?"

"Well, they played a song out it for me."

"And am I supposed to feel glad?"

"I'll sing it. We'll dance."

"Dance to you singing?"

"Sure, hold out your arms."

"This is silly. I think dancin' is a sin."

"It ain't silly, it's fun," he said.

"Leonard!" Frances put on a sour face.

"Okay, I'll let it go."

O O O

Leonard would have his shirt off and in his undershirt he would stand next to Frances after supper and dry the dishes she handed to him. He still might have a little fragrance of sawdust from the sawmill, but it was a fresh, piney, clean kind of a smell. It made the house complete, she thought.

"I just love the moonlight, don't you, Leonard?" Usually they moved to the porch after supper, with the house dark inside, now she sat on the edge of the porch with her feet on the top step and Leonard on the step below that. It was true that Tallahatta was bathed in silver. "It makes the pines out there look like they are castles. See the castles?"

But Leonard was in a very sober mood, not in a castle mood. His sense of responsibility for being a husband had fallen on him more than ever for the past several weeks now, and he was setting foot on the bridge between his late boyhood and his full manhood and the realization that he had taken on another person to care for. That bridge in his mind seemed somewhat shaky. It wasn't easy to put a foot down.

So he looked far off and said quietly, "I ain't done right by you, Frances."

"I'm happy."

"I know you need more."

"But what more do I need?"

"Oh, comfort."

"But, Leonard. Look. Look around."

"All I see is a busted-down half-farm and a busted-down spraddle-roof house."

Frances leaned and wrapped her arms around Leonard's shoulders and lay her head next to his.

"I see it. It's pretty."

"It's got to be better, Frances."

"Know how you could make it better, Leonard?"

"No. How?"

"Kiss me."

"Kiss you?"

"Kiss me like we was little kids. Just a peck. Right here." Frances tapped a finger on a cheek. "I dream about you, Leonard. You know those old knights like they had in the old days?"

"I'm your knight?"

"Well, you sure are. You ride around on a horse."

"Horse? Where am I going?"

"Oh, I don't know where you are going. Do you have to be going someplace?"

"Well, if I'm your knight I have to be going someplace." Leonard stood up and stepped down off the porch. He was in his undershirt and moonlight poured over his shoulders. He stretched out his arms, "Sir Lion!" he shouted and whirled in a circle then roared a big lion-roar just to be funny and then he whinnied like a horse and shouted "GIDDYAP!"

"Oh, Leonard, you making fun of me?"

"No, Frances." Leonard came back to the porch and lay with his head in Frances' lap.

"You know what I'm thinking, Frances?"

"What, Leonard Cassity?" She hadn't stopped giggling.

"I'm thinking I'm the luckiest man in Tallahatta Springs, Alabama."

"Leonard, there ain't hardly anybody in Tallahatta Springs."

"Then I'm the luckiest man in the world."

"That's what you are, Leonard Cassity. You're the luckiest man in the world."

"That's right. The world. Luckiest man in the world."

And Leonard said no more. And Leonard decided he would steal a car for Frances as soon as the opportunity came along..

SEVEN

W<small>HEN</small> M<small>ISS</small> H<small>EARN</small> ARRIVED AT work, and she was always on time, William Harold the Third was already in his office working on numbers. The profit would be modest but it would be a profit. At the weekly meeting with Francis X. Harold, Francis X. would nod his head. Probably, it was too soon to know what Aaron Silverstein's response to the Gordon property would be. Nevertheless, Mister Harold seemed to grow noticeably more tense and on the street he found himself greeted by inquiring looks that were not accompanied by words. He had nothing to report to Francis X. Harold today concerning the potential lease. Perhaps he had made a mistake by making such a show of the visit by the George Washington's All-American stores.

William Harold the Third emerged, handed two pages of penciled numbers to Miss Hearn for typing, returned to his office and closed the door. Twenty-five minutes later he re-emerged, his jacket on, took the typed pages and left the bank. Miss Hearn pulled the book of daily inspirations from a drawer and clamped a pencil in her jaw. "Putting others above self" sometimes came with difficulty to her and she turned pages. She had seen something that said it wasn't necessarily a flaw. Or she thought she had, in one way or another.

"I say 'is Mister Harold in?' Aaron Silverstein repeated. "I think you must have a gift for concentration."

"Mister Silverstein?"

"I think so. Yes," said Mister Silverstein.

"School," yelped Miss Hearn guiltily. "School does it. I'm sorry." How long had he been standing there? It had been more than two weeks since the tour of the store.

"You missed him. Just barely. He's gone to his weekly meeting with the chairman. Until noon. You're here."

"I am. And I have decided to lease."

"Yes," said Miss Hearn. "I mean, *yes!*" and Miss Hearn pumped a fist in the air.

"You seem pleased," Aaron Silverstein observed.

Miss Hearn stood and held out a hand. "Mister Silverstein, I could not be more pleased, and Thomasville welcomes you."

"My pleasure. If he is out, perhaps I can use the time another way until he returns. If you could direct me to Mister Harrigan, the insurance man?"

"Oh-h-h."

"Also out?"

"I mean Mister Harrigan was here about an hour ago and made a deposit. Then he left to go to the baseball field to try out a new pitcher. He was in his baseball suit."

"Uniform."

"Yes. And he owns the team, taking the risk, and is its manager, and is a player as well. He does this to boost the community. The Clarke County Democrats give the community pep, The team travels. To prove the need for roads, boosting the community. I firmly stand behind him in this. Boosting promotes development."

"Needed."

"Yes. And pitching is important. The new pitcher is important."

"Very."

"I do not know if you know baseball but I know you know politics and I will say pitching is as important as voting. Or nearly."

"In Chicago I go to about half the White Socks' home games every year."

"Oh-h-h. The White Socks."

"Yes?"

"Wasn't that the bad team?"

"And what is 'bad', Miss Hearn? The players were terribly underpaid. Yet they were the best players in the game. Do you suppose you could direct me to the baseball field? Perhaps we could find a minute to talk about insurance."

"Yes, and you go down that way. And excuse me for pointing. And should we walk to the door?"

"I think so."

On the sidewalk Miss Hearn pointed again and said "and don't count the alley as a street. Third street. Turn right. It's not far. You will see the stands."

"Yes."

"Yes. And Mister Silverstein…."

"Speaking frankly again?"

"Please. And Mister Silverstein, George Washington's All-America stores will be very happy here in Thomasville."

"George Washington's happiness is my happiness. Do you attend the games?"

"I miss none. And Mister Silverstein, you should smile like that more. I think it brings out the inner you."

"My duty to my inner me."

"Of course. Now don't count the alley."

Miss Hearn watched as Aaron Silverstein drove down the street turned right into the alley then backed out and resumed.

Inside Miss Hearn went into Mr. Harold's office and closed the door. She tilted back in the chair. He would not be back before noon.

Her father had pulled some strings to get her this job. He, like everyone, knew the stories of the lean halfback of 1914 intramural football who made legendary dashes around end. They tried to lure him to the varsity with prospects of travel to other places to play. The Crimson Tide. To Texas or Kansas but he remained steadfast to the Delta Kappa Epsilons and even now, this long after graduation his waistline remained trim and he looked good in his bankers' blues.

But he was the same man who bought his suits with two pairs of trousers. One pair to become shiny in the seat at the office and the other pair to wear to his weekly meetings with the chairman of the bank. Security was a very uninspiring virtue. Why bother to look for it?

On the other hand was this man whose trousers were a crazy zig zag, open- collared but mysterious and deep. Much more deep.

What did she know?

What could she know?

About men?

Miss Hearn went to the cabinets and began to lay out the various forms for lease transactions on Mister Harold's desk. This afternoon two minds would clash. She was female. She was a graduate of the Mississippi State College for Women. For *women*. This was the moment nature had made her for. This was her moment of selection.

EIGHT

The "correction" idea began when Aaron Silverstein the morning after Silverstein rolled into town on Friday evening and checked in at the only hotel, which was the floor above the town drugstore. The hotel consisted of four rooms and a bath at the end of the hall. The hotel was mostly used by lumber people from up north who came to town once or twice a year to buy lumber and who stayed in town as briefly as they possibly could. Silverstein had the entire floor to himself.

In the morning he bathed in the rusty iron bathtub and dressed and walked down the street to Win Harrigan's insurance office at the far end of the block. He would sign and pay for the insurance policy he bought to cover the store.

Silverstein found a note taped to the door saying that Win Harrigan had gone to morning baseball practice and would return after lunch.

In the afternoon, however, Silverstein had an appointment to interview a Mrs. Theodosia Gordon for the position of head seamstress and floor manager. Mrs. Gordon had been recommended to him in a very nice note he received at his office from a lady who owned the florist and gift shop on Main Street. She apparently had been the previous owner, had been through difficulties, but wished now to be back in the world of business.

Silverstein knew the way to the park and he found Win Harrigan standing behind third base with a fungo bat, hitting fly balls to the outfielders. He took a seat in the stands and watched. Someone muffed a fly ball, another returned balls wildly to Win Harrigan, but all in all there seemed to be three or so competent outfielders. Alongside first base a slender young man who was apparently wearing a suit of red flannel underwear beneath a sleeveless sweatshirt threw balls to a catcher who gestured back with his hands and wrist to emulate a pitching motion. The young man nodded then threw the next pitch. Silverstein guessed he was learning to throw the curve.

In a few minutes Silverstein caught Win Harrigan's eye and the manager laid down the bat and walked to the stands.

Silverstein glanced at the policy and signed it and wrote a check.

"Team?" he asked.

"We call us the Clarke County Democrats. Some of us can play a little."

"You?"

"If I have to. Manage."

"Takes brains."

"Ask next door. They may be over there."

Silverstein smiled.

"Do you win?"

"Oh, yes, we win."

"I mean *always* win. *Must* you win? Sometimes you lose. You might lose."

"We could lose anytime. Anytime we play. Do you mean lose *purposely?*

"Accidentally, more or less."

"How lose *accidentally?*"

"Errors. Strikeouts. Crucial mistakes. Baseball is full of that."

"Bad fortune strikes. Happens to the best of teams."

"Suppose…. Suppose…that if someone had bet on you to win and then you lost?"

"The person who'd made that bet would lose also."

"But the other gambler would win."

"Like the Black Socks?"

"The Black Socks were horribly maligned. Charles Comiskey paid them next to nothing."

"The gambler won a lot of money. What was his name?"

"Rothstein. But it wasn't simply about the money."

"What was it about?"

"The feeling."

"Feeling of what?"

"Of power. And control. The outcome of the Series. That was the greatest sporting event in the world. 'The World Series.' He controlled the outcome. That is the greatest feeling in the world. To a gambler. It is better than the money."

"We play to boost the town. I'm the chairman of the booster committee. In a year or two we may be in a league. League like the Tri-State League. Big crowds."

"But you'd like to make a little money for the team."

"Uniforms. Better uniforms."

"Yes. Now suppose…. Suppose you lost a few games in the season and someone had bet on you to win?"

"You say we would fix the games?"

"It's a bad word to use. There's a Yiddish word, *farrikhtn*, it means to "fix," yes, but it means it in the sense of 'to repair' or 'to correct'. You would 'correct' the score to meet certain limits, which we would know about, just you and I."

"There would have to be others."

"Yes, of course. Trusted others. And I would want these others to realize something for their effort. You could have yours as well. And also a certain amount to benefit the team."

"Not all my players would."

"Several?"

"Three. Four. Third base. First base. Catcher. An outfielder."

"Enough. The White Socks had only eight. But three, four in key positions. Pitcher? What about the young man in the red flannels over there throwing to your catcher?"

Win Harrigan chuckled. "The long underwear. He complains that he's cold. He complains that he has a stomach ache. He complains about many things. Still, he may well be the next Christy Matthewson. We're teaching him the curve right now. Nearly unhittable with the fast ball. But no."

"What about that business manager? The banker fellow?"

"Not. Definitely not. Keep it away from him. Too idealistic. Never got over college. You know, 'rah! rah! Give all for the fraternity. Still the college boy. Won't even run the bank himself. Every week he goes out to kiss his uncle's back end. That girl he hired will be vice president herself the first time she ever gets to see the old man. But Harold is right about one thing."

"That is?"

"The sport is coming into its Golden Age. Teams. Players. Ruth. Amazing. The stands love it. Leagues, they will all double in ten years. Do you know that Omaha against White Autos for the amateur championship drew a hundred and fifteen thousand a couple of years ago? In a year or two we may be in a league. Some Big League team may pay us to develop players for them. Changing the subject, how will we each know what the 'correct' score is supposed to be?"

"Western Union. I will just need a few days in advance to set up the action. I think you'll see what that feeling is. You control all of it. Don't think there isn't plenty of this in baseball. I'll estimate what the action will be and telegraph you. Let me know about the players. When I'm back you might give me some figures for insuring the other stores."

"Be my pleasure."

"'Clarke County Democrats'. Good. Good for us all. I think this is going to be a good thing."

○ ○ ○

The team had a road game against the military school cadets. All the cadets' parents had money. As the children of parents with money The baseball squad insulted the Democrats.

In the top of the eighth Leonard lead off for the Democrats. The Dems trailed three to two but Leonard had a good feeling.

The Cadets, almighty, insufferable, and invincible, scored all their runs in the second inning when Leonard gave up a triple, two doubles and a single, a big inning for them. But after that, Leonard settled down. It was a good day. Hot. But that helped him. In the first two innings he wore a sweatshirt under his flannel uniform and now that he was sweating it lay across the back of the bench. He had begun to strike out batters. *Made to play this game*, he mumbled to himself and threw a fastball that jumped up in the hitter's eyes. *Money in the bank*. After the second he'd held them scoreless and he had seven strikeouts and no walks.

The Democrats' runs came when Leonard walked in the third, and then scored two batters later on a hard groundout by Questionable. Medicine Men added the other run in the fourth but two men died on base.

On the bench Leonard wore an old jacket to keep his pitching arm warm. He took it off and walked to the plate. He felt cooler but it was still hot and Leonard had picked up a burn because the visitor bench had no cover. The home bench had a shed. "Step in, batter," said the umpire.

The Cadet pitcher went into a prolonged arm-twirling windup and delivered a curve that began to arc about halfway to the plate and ended up about a foot away from the outside part of the plate. Leonard's curves broke tightly and at the last instant.

"Strike," said the umpire. Leonard stepped away from the plate, swung the bat loosely and stepped back in.

The Cadet pitcher wound up again and this time it was a fastball, again outside but this time also below Leonard's knees. "Strike," said the umpire.

Leonard stepped out of the batter's box again. "Outside and low," he said, but he did not look back.

"It's nearly suppertime so don't look for anything back here," said a voice in return.

"Crybaby," said a second voice. That was the catcher.

Leonard knew that on the next pitch he would be called out. He moved back into the batter's box. "Come on, Mister Pitcher, come on," he whispered to himself. "Come on."

It would have been a strike, across the middle and belt high. Leonard turned quickly, smoothly and his hips opened squarely to the pitcher. Propelled by his wrists the bat reached a flat level plane. and the fattest part made contact with the ball just in front of the plate.

God!

"God!" he yelped.

The ball rocketed over the third baseman's head, landed two feet fair and rolled to the corner. Rounding first Leonard saw the left fielder retrieve the ball at the fence, saw the shortstop move into short left field to take the throw and felt the second baseman breathing behind his right shoulder as Leonard came to second base standing up. "Nice hit, turd," said the second baseman and went back to his position. A none out standup double. Now the Dems were in business.

Leonard hit ninth. Medicine Men would be up.

Leonard had never before prayed to the Baseball King but he looked toward the bench and could see a wisp of smoke rising from a pile of small sticks. *Funny ain't it?* he thought as he lead off second, *Jesus don't give a hoot about baseball but the Baseball King does.* The fire may not have been started soon enough because on the second pitch Medicine Men popped out to the catcher.

Bringing Medicine Men to the plate.

Stubby, patient, Medicine Men took two strikes then leaned over the plate and into a curve ball. He made a show of writhing on the ground. The umpire had no choice but to award first base.

Doctor Pearlington came to bat for the fourth time. He had flied to left and struck out twice. On the second pitch he topped a ball that rolled between the pitcher and third base and the pitcher made a move to field it. So did the third baseman.

The pitcher looked to third base hoping to find the shortstop there and make the force out on Leonard, but the shortstop hadn't covered the base. When he turned to first, Doctor Pearlington was nearly across it safe. Leonard was safe at third and Medicine Men stood at second. Bases loaded, just one out.

Richie, the earnest high school player, came to bat.

Leonard watched as Richie hit a sky high fly that the second baseman caught two steps on the infield grass. No baserunner moved. Two out.

Leonard could still be optimistic. The next hitter was Questionable.

Questionable had played some organized ball. Someone said he even played a few games in the Big Leagues during the personnel shortage caused by the War. He had doubled in the first and grounded out twice but had hit the ball hard each time. One of the outs drove in Leonard's run.

Questionable had his bat and stood in the batter's box.

Win Harrigan on the bench called out "Time" to the umpire and came off the bench. "Time," he said again.

What was this?

Leonard heard Mister Harrigan say to the umpire "injured player," and then say "Buckles."

Injury? What injury? Leonard didn't see any injury. Buckles? Buckles would strike out.

"Wait!" called Leonard from third base. "You can't...."

Leonard watched as Buckles swung wildly at three pitches which no other hitter would ever have swung at.

◯ ◯ ◯

After the game Leonard got off the bus where Mister Harrigan parked it in Thomasville and walked the two miles home to Tallahatta Springs.

Leonard ate his supper in his baseball uniform and said nothing and Frances said nothing to him.

After he ate he went to the porch and leaned against the shaky column and looked at the bleak field of stumps until the sun set behind the wood. When it got too dark to see Leonard stood and stripped off the uniform leaving it damp in a pile on the floor. He called Frances in a low voice.

"Frances."

Leonard led Frances by the hand the twenty feet to the pump where he sat legs crossed Indian-style under the spout. He made Frances pump cold water over his shoulders and back for ten minutes. "Leonard," she said, "can I stop this?"

"Pump it," he said.

All the ground around the pump was mud, Leonard was sitting in mud; he stood and shivered.

"You need towels." Frances went to the house, returned and wrapped Leonard's shaking body with two towels.

"I'm cold," he said.

"Was it bad?"

"It weren't nothing."

When they were in the house Leonard said "get me a blanket, will you?"

Frances had already put away the blankets for the summer but she left and came back with a blanket and lay it across Leonard's shaking body under the sheet.

"Leonard, it couldn't have been good."

"It was good."

"I want you to tell me the truth."

"I lost."

"Is that all? Every team loses."

"I guess so."

"And there ain't no reason for it to be. You told me that yourself."

"Must not be."

"Leonard, why are you acting this way?

"Why would they take a good player out and put in a bad one?"

She started to say she did not know, but she heard Leonard snore gently. "Little baby," she said so she changed to her nightshirt and crawled into bed next to him to keep him warm.

Tallahatta Springs, Alabama
Saturday, July 10, 1920

Dear Mother Cassity

Leonard got saved last Sunday but it was not from nothing I had done unless I prayed for this way without my knowing it. Leonard was pitching and he said he threw a ball harder than he had ever thrown in his life. It went like a rocket but it hit the other young man in the head. Leonard ran down to where he was laying on the ground. Right there on his knees in the dirt he told Jesus he would take him as his Lord and Savior if he would bring the young man back. In a few minutes this young man began to stir again and in a few minutes he was alright. But Leonard says it taught him you can do nothing without Jesus. Leonard gives thanks at the table now and gets on his knees before bed. We will miss the $6.00 but we know not having it is Jesuses way of saying we are blessed. I thank you for forgiving me.

Your loving daughter
Frances Cassity

P.S. We may expect.

Hitting the batter made Leonard lose track of himself inwardly. He seemed unlike himself for days. Not morose, just pensive, willing to talk, but not much, he sat on the porch his back to the shaky column and looked out at the field of stumps. Other times when he did that he usually sat and looked, but now once or twice he got up and walked among them, where Frances held her tea parties with Mister Frazzletop and Mister Armaround, and Mister Low and Mister Unhappy. Of course Leonard did not know about the tea parties and the poke bonnet and Frances watched from the window and wondered what he was thinking.

On Thursday night Leonard said to Frances, "I don't know, Jesus is pushing me toward you."

"That's funny," said Frances, "you ain't moving at all."

"I don't mean that. I mean he's pushing me toward you."

"Wait a minute, Leonard."

Frances went away and then came back.

"What is that?" Leonard asked.

"It's a dress."

"I know that."

"Me'n Fergie made it."

"It's beautiful."

"Well, you know, Mister Ferguson owns the feed and seed store."

"I know that."

"It all comes in sacks and a lot of the sacks are just beautiful, flowers or designs printed on them. You wash them and you have the material. Ladies can use the material to make their dresses. Fergie had this pattern."

"It was a sack?"

"See?" Frances twirled. "Fergie has a sewing machine. Sundays when you played ball we went to her house after church and sewed."

"Frances, maybe I ain't supposed to feel this way. I mean…so much. I know we…you know what I mean…but since I been saved I got a different feeling about it….It's like Jesus is telling me to… give me a feeling to… so you think Jesus should be telling me to do that? I have these desires at night. I don't know if I ought to."

"Have them, Leonard. Touch me."

"It's a powerful dress."

"Fergie said it makes me look pretty. Don't you think Jesus tells me some things sometimes, Leonard? Pushes me toward you? Makes me desire you? Can you remember whether our first kiss was vanilla or chocolate?"

"Chocolate."

"Vanilla. Do you know Jesus tells me that Leonard Cassity, Junior, will be someone great? Feel me push on you?" Frances pressed her body against Leonard's. "Touch me, Leonard."

"I don't know that I have to talk about it anymore, Frances. Right now, at least."

"Can you be a little more careful with this dress, Leonard? It took me half an afternoon to sew that just right. *Leonard!* Leonard, don't think I'm going anywhere."

○ ○ ○

And after Leonard got saved the Holy Ghost began to prosecute him. To convict him of the sins of the world, to convince him of his sin, to convict him of falling short.

Leonard became convinced the Holy Ghost aimed to rebuke him for ever playing on Sundays. The rebukes showed themselves in some exotic ways.

First it showed itself as a religious lust, a carnal fever that he could not understand. He knew that Frances never would. He pursued Frances around the house in the evening, having deep urges of the kind that he had told her about. They came along anytime. As he dried the dishes; or they came on him a little later when he cornered her on the porch. Once he brought her into the yard saying "you're my chicken and I am the rooster." That time, as Frances heated water for a second bath that night, she said "Leonard. Leonard, try and act civilized. I've got nothing but red clay down my back." But God made it clear to Leonard that he was made for Frances and that they were one.

One night he complained about the house.

"It ain't on a hill," he said.

"It's on a little hill," Frances replied.

"You ought to be living in a house on a hill, Frances," Leonard said. "People who have come up in the world live like that." He had not done enough.

Next he walked to town after work and bought a twelve-foot ladder at the hardware. He bargained with the hardware owner until the owner made less than a dollar on the transaction then he demanded that the owner deliver the ladder in his truck to the house at Tallahatta.

He bought white paint and began to paint the house from the roof down but the builders had never painted the house and the house was fifty years old and the thirsty wood drank up the paint leaving the boards a dingy gray. So Leonard stopped the painting after he had painted the house about four feet down from the roof.

Worse, he had been breaking God's law by playing baseball on Sunday and so he quit the team.

The result was a disaster for the Clarke County Democrats. The team had two games left to play and it lost them both by big scores. The game following the hit batter incident Leonard was on the mound when he felt the Holy Ghost enter into him. In the second inning he became so rattled Fingers had to relieve him and the opponents scored fourteen runs. After the game he gave Win Harrigan his uniform and he did not show up for the last game of the season.

That Sunday he spent in church sitting next to Frances.

As the starting pitcher in the final game now desperate Win Harrigan lost also.

The team ended the 1920 season with their record at five and two. But the two losses hung heavily on the team and on the town, too. They were filled with portent. There was no promise that 1921 would offer anything better.

Leonard thought that he should feel happy because he had satisfied God, and Jesus his only son. The Holy Ghost had told him his marriage permitted no compromises. No compromises whatever. God had given him Frances to make happy. He thought he should have felt happy.

But inwardly he felt nothing. If anything, dissatisfaction.

He did not feel happy at all.

NINE

Meridian, Mississippi
July 6, 1921

Mister Charles Comiskey
President, Chicago White Sox
Baseball Club
Comiskey Park
Chicago, Illinois

Dear Mister Comiskey:

There is a pitcher down here playing for the Clarke
County Democrats in Alabama that I think you should
be aware of. He is about 22 years of age and has a
fastball with major league velocity on it. He also has
a respectable curve which he uses effectively.

Last Sunday I witnessed him throw a no-hitter at
the Meridian Fire House Team. This is a team which
incorporates some very good batting.

I know you are making a valiant effort to rebuild the club after the disaster coming from the 1919 Series and that the coming trial will be anguishing for you. Replacing Eddie Cicotte and Lefty Williams will be a challenge that no club owner would desire.

The era of the new "lively" ball may mean that some baseball players might hit twenty, or twenty-five or perhaps even thirty home runs in a single year, and the clubs must find means to counter this new threat.

Because of their win over the Fire House team, the Clarke County Democrats now seem certain to play the M&O Firebox Stokers in their annual "Casey Jones Classic," a three day event. The Stokers gather their talent from up and down the whole line and they would give even some big league teams a day they would wish they hadn't seen.

Meridian is a town not hard to reach. It is simply south on the IC railroad to Jackson and then by the Vicksburg Road to Meridian. Hotels here are very good.

If not you in person, then someone from management definitely ought to look at this prospect.

With best wishes,

Your scout
Foster Hawkins.

O O O

Someone should have been able to offer an accurate account of the final two outs of the no-hitter, but no one apparently could. And five hundred people sat in the stands. People scoffed at what spectators said later about the play and sneered and told them they had suffered sunstroke or something like it.

"The Tree's", or "Oak's," or Hogarth's line drive should have gone into left field, driving home the two base runners and making the score two to one in favor of the Meridian Fire House team, ending the game and ruining Leonard's no-hit game. No one wanted to say it was a "supernatural" event, but that seemed to be the only way to describe it.

Some said The Tree's bat shattered into a thousand pieces and that slowed the drive down, then it miraculously put itself back together again. That vision appeared among fans at opposite ends of the grandstand who had not spoken to one another. Other spectators said the bat did not shatter at all. Some of those who said the bat shattered later amended the statement to say that it "sounded like" the bat shattered into a thousand pieces but the ball left the bat like a rocket.

Leonard saw the Holy Ghost make the throw for the final out. He saw the dove descend and lift the ball from Medicine Men's glove and throw it to first base in a roar of wind. Then the dove ascended to heaven again. Leonard alone saw the dove, but almost everyone in the stands heard a roar of wind.

Medicine Men knew that the Baseball King built him a glass throne which he ascended to snare the drive in the web of his glove. Then, five feet above the turf, he planted his feet on the glass throne and made a furious throw that he otherwise could not have made, over to first base to complete the double play. Except for one or two, everyone saw him plant his feet on something that was not there.

Foster Hawkins, the Chicago White Sox scout, saw it as it probably really happened. On his scorecard he wrote "F-6" for a flyout to shortstop on a weak line drive by The Tree making out number two in the inning, and "6-3" next to the runner at first for an assisted putout at first base, and out number three that finished the inning and the game and then he put his papers away and went home to write a letter. He had recorded every pitch Leonard Cassity had thrown, curves, fastballs, balls, strikes.

The game seemed routine for the first six innings. Meridian Fire House had no hits, but that wasn't altogether noteworthy. They might rally anytime.

The Democrats scored one run in the third on three consecutive singles and that was enough to keep Leonard comfortable. Leonard always felt comfortable with any kind of a lead.

In the seventh it became clear that Leonard had to collect nine more outs without giving up a hit and some suspense began to gather on both benches. Leonard's players left him alone and didn't speak to him. He sat at the far end of the bench in the leather bomber's jacket his father had given him after buying it from an ex-private who had stolen it from an American pilot in France when the pilot went into town on leave. Leonard made it through the seventh.

In the eighth he began to get the jitters. He had never come this close before.

Fortunately the weak part of the lineup came to bat, but even the weak batters began to go two balls up on him. Constable called time twice and walked out. Win Harrigan joined him the second time. "Take your time, Lenny," he said in a calm, fatherly way. He never called Leonard "Lenny". Leonard said "I will. But I'm not feeling good. Should I leave?"

"The game?"

"My belly."

"Leave the game while you're ahead?"

"I guess not." It came to Leonard that if he could do it while he was not feeling good, he could do it anytime. "These hitters cant even touch your hot stuff, Leonard," said Win Harrigan. "They don't even have the balls of a mouse." The umpire began to walk toward the mound. "I'd stick you in there against Ruth."

"Yes, sir," said Leonard and then he prowled around the back of the mound studying how his belly felt. Finally the umpire called out to him "play ball, son," and then he set down the side on groundouts.

In their half of the ninth the Democrats did nothing again and the team took the field for the home ninth. Still no hits recorded against Leonard and the one run lead held. But Leonard had to face the top of the batting order. Nobody on that Meridian Fire House team could ever remember being held hitless for an entire game. Leonard began to hear insults. Frustrated insults. Doctor Pearlington stood five feet six inches tall and walked and ran with a sort of militant duck waddle with his back end sticking out. Leonard's sawmill co-worker, Cobb, said Pearlington would "have to stand on a bucket to kick himself in the ass." As the town pharmacist, he knew he played the game to vent a bellicose nature that practicing pharmacy wouldn't allow for. Doctor Pearlington walked from third base to the coach's box and took his hand from his glove. He held up a fist "Shove this up your ass," he said and went back to his position.

"What did you say?" said a voice politely from the bench.

Doctor Pearlington walked over again and took his hand from the glove. "I said shove this up your ass."

"You shove it up your ass, too," said another voice from the bench.

The umpire walked over and pointed a finger at someone. "And you shove it up your ass, too, umpire," said a third voice and the umpire's thumb went up.

Leonard by then had completed his warmup pitches.

TEN

A BLESSED DAY, FRANCES THOUGHT. THE warmest day so far in this already warm April of 1921, she looked at the blue sky on the short journey to the pump for Leonard junior's bath water.

Over with, too! That month-long stay in town in the last days of her pregnancy to be near her mother and the doctor. A memory, the startled awakening in the middle of the night; forgotten in the joy of motherhood, the pain, the commotion, the thrill, Doctor Cranford who still smelled like bourbon in the early morning hour; the demanding cry, and the release. Her son.

Leonard could not stay in town. He had to work. He remained at the house in Tallahatta Springs and made his own meals.

Frances walked to the pump, turning back to take in the house, there with its white paint job, which descended by only about four feet from the eaves, trailing off in the boards above the windows in random licks. It was the paint job that stopped where Leonard stopped. That was the part about Leonard that exasperated her. He could get hot about something then cool down, but you never knew what he was thinking. Leonard got tired of the house just drinking up paint. The house wouldn't bend to him so he ceased to fight it. He would have to outsmart the house. He spent nights after supper talking about his next move versus the paint. *Planning, planning, planning,* she thought. *Always planning. He'll master himself and get back at it.* And it really didn't matter. The next house is over a half a mile away. Nobody sees it. She sighed.

But what to do with this wonderfully warm day? With their lives, hers and Leonard Junior's? She turned in the other direction.

Between the pump and the privy lay a small stretch of bare ground, a rectangle about twenty feet by thirty feet. *That will make a fine garden,* she thought.

Yes. Fresh vegetables all summer long!

Tomatoes, some beans on poles, *Mmnn.* Field peas to shell. Hills of squash. Okra. Watermelons, *in a tub, in that cold pump water.* She could plant and tend to all that. And by herself, and with Leonard Junior in his wicker basket beside her at the end of a row. 'Course, she'd have to have Leonard buy her a shovel and a rake and a hoe but she could shovel up the ground. But he would come home from work and the plot would be more and more complete. Frances Smith Cassity, mistress of her own garden.

The April sun had begun to bring out the freckles on her nose. When I'm older the freckles will go away. *They make me look like a young girl.* I'll need the poke bonnet even today. But, if the poke bonnet, *then it's a tea party!* And that's what she would do with their lives today.

On the dining room table she lay Leonard Junior in his wicker basket and covered him with his blue blanket. She put two folded diapers on his tummy.

She packed the tea party in another basket. Teapot. Cups. Saucers. A checked tablecloth. Then from a drawer, her grandmother's poke bonnet, and she tied it beneath her chin.

A basket in each hand she left the porch and a walked down to the pine stumps, to Mister Frazzletop and Mister Armaround and Mister Low and she spread the tablecloth across Mister Low and set out the cups.

When she was little she never had real tea, not really, just pretend tea, so there was no reason to change that. Now she poured the tea.

"May I pour you some tea, Mister Frazzletop?" she asked.

"Thank you," said Mister Frazzletop. He had never spoken before.

"Frances, will you need to nurse Leonard while you are here?" asked Mister Armaround.

Wide-eyed, confused and uncomfortable now, Frances answered "I think so. You're speaking," she added.

"We're your guests, so shouldn't we?" asked Frazzletop. "Isn't that the fun of a party?"

"Oh, yes," answered Frances. "I'm pleased that you're speaking."

"If you're nursing Leonard Junior you might like to nestle in the crook of my arm," Armaround said. "You might be more comfortable."

Frances wiggled sideways and settled in the crooked root that had been pulled up when the tree fell. She said "thank you."

"You're warm," said Armaround.

"Frances…." Said Frazzletop, then paused. He spoke deliberately and with a serious tone. Frazzletop had a deep and unhurried voice. He might have been an uncle. "Frances…." He started again. "Frances, are we too personal if we ask why we see Leonard on the porch each evening leaning on the column and looking at the trees until it's too dark to see?"

"He's withdrawn," said Frances. "He's not at peace with himself."

"Do you know why?"

"I'm not sure."

"Leonard is searching. Sometimes men get lost," said Frazzletop.

"But what is he searching for? Frances seemed puzzled.

"His connection to you."

"Hoot-not-giving," said a voice that seemed to come from under the tablecloth.

"But I am not searching," Frances insisted.

"Yes, you are. But you do not know it."

"You know this?'

"Trees are special," said Frazzletop. "To you, knowing comes when you are awake. Or even in dreams and visions. But to us, knowing comes through our connection to the earth. If people understood trees, they would understand the connectedness of all life. In a sense, we *are* life to you. We provide the oxygen you breathe."

"But people are special" said Frances.

"We see how Christian you are, Frances," Frazzletop said. "But think. The tree was the last disciple of Christ, with him to the end. He carried one of us to his death."

"Deep-water unquenchable love," said the voice from under the cloth.

"Who is that?" asked Frances.

"Mister Low," said Frazzletop. "The tree-cutter took too much of him. He's not all there, as they say." Mister Armaround laughed. "Now he speaks only in compound adjectives. He became a university."

"But to go on," said Frazzletop, "so that you will understand. At the Crucifixion all the disciples except John fled in fear. But one of us, a tree, became his servant. Felt his blood in our pores. Felt him take his last breath. For this, certain things are given to us. We know your life, past, present and future. And Leonard's too."

"And what will become of us?"

"That."

"Then, what will?"

"We are not given that to say."

"Will we become connected?"

"One day."

"Once-married unity," said the voice under the tablecloth.

"You shouldn't object if Leonard plays baseball, Frances," said Frazzletop.

"Even on Sunday?"

"Love unites you, Frances. Not a rule about Sunday. As long as you have Leonard you must keep him near to you."

"Why do you say 'as long as I have him'?"

"Deep-watered love," said low from under the cloth. "Tree-strong Frances," he said after that.

"Trees can feel love. It is to us as oxygen is to you. It is the exchange we make with humanity. A gift to us for sharing the pain of the Crucifixion. It is what we felt in the blood of Jesus at Calvary. But, Frances, we will not tell you this ever again. We have simply wanted to tell you how strong love is and that there is nothing else. You must always know that you, Frances, are first in his heart. First in Leonard's heart and will be always. Always."

The same Friday in April Frances gave her tea party for the pine stumps, Aaron Silverstein spent in his office looking over timetables. The rebuilt White Sox, if that was the term for them, opened the season April 21 at Comiskey Park against the Tigers. And Frank Navin, the Tigers owner, had hired that demented outfielder of theirs, Ty Cobb, to a contract as player-manager, and Aaron Silverstein planned to be in the stands.

The time had also come to order the summer merchandise for the George Washington's All American stores and so Aaron Silverstein had to visit the Sears Roebuck warehouses and select merchandise to be light-fingered away by the warehousemen who pilfered everything for him. Last year with the cooperation of Win Harrigan's third baseman, his first baseman, and catcher, he had been able to *farrikhtn*[1] two of the Clarke County Democrats' games.

Not many, but they had been enough to provide him with sufficient gambling winnings that he now could very nearly pay the warehouse thieves with free cash for all the summer merchandise they would steal from Sears for his growing chain. All in all Aaron Silverstein felt successful in business.

Aaron Silverstein missed his old friends. He wanted to catch up. He missed the sidewalks and the awnings over them, and so crowded with merchandise people had to walk in the streets. He missed all that. Finally he admitted to himself the real reason for his visit to Chicago. He intended to pursue marriage with Miss Hearn and he had no idea how to carry out a courtship. He needed advice.

The following Monday he checked his bags aboard the Alabama and Vicksburg's noon train to Jackson to connect with the Illinois Central's Panama Limited up from New Orleans.

Both trains, the north- and the southbound Panama Limiteds, all Pullman, no coaches, departed their stations at New Orleans and Chicago

---

1   Yiddish, "to correct". In this case for the team to "correct" the final score to a prearranged outcome to better the gambling odds.

at the same hour daily, twelve-thirty p.m. The two would thunder past one another in opposite directions at Fulton, Kentucky, south of Louisville on their overnight journeys. With barbers and ladies' maids and fine dining aboard they gave passengers an experience in luxury train travel. Each arrived at its destination before noon the following day.

At four-forty-four the northbound Panama arrived at Jackson, Mississippi, with four minutes to make up. Tomorrow it would arrive at Central Station on Michigan Avenue and Aaron Silverstein would be home. Tonight he planned to read and be comfortable.

Aaron Silverstein unrolled his copies of the *Sporting News*. The tabloid bible of baseball arrived in his office rolled in brown paper. Given the mails it was always a week or more late but tonight he could catch up. Tomorrow he would learn the news on the street. He would learn about the Black Sox trial. The trial would begin in July.

All journalists were liars and bribe-takers or they wouldn't be journalists but the *Sporting News*' were less so. The trial would be fixed or there wouldn't be a trial. It was Chicago. But he saw nothing between the lines.

◗ ◗ ◗

About the White Sox he read that Eddie Collins joined training camp late, but he had been working out with the University of Pennsylvania squad. He learned that Charles Comiskey had made some trades and the pitching was now good, bad and worse and he knew that Comiskey had no hope of replacing the indicted pitchers, Eddie Cicotte and Lefty Williams, and so the Sox could only look to a dismal season ahead.

For the remainder of the evening Aaron Silverstein treated treated himself to some of the cuisine New Orleans was famous for. He enjoyed some cold oysters on the half shell, some others in a sauce and a fillet of trout smothered in flakes of almonds and some dark, impenetrable coffee.

He had made an appointment with the barber for a shampoo and a haircut. He wished he could get rid of this dandruff. Around nine he called for the porter to make up his berth, handed over his suits to the valet to be cleaned and pressed, and then he read some more of the *Sporting News*. At ten he turned out the light. He slept peacefully, feeling the iron wheels on iron rails lulling his tired back.

He woke a little before eight with the train near Champaign and he had breakfast on white linens with more of that impenetrable coffee and he watched the Illinois prairies roll by, now new and green, in his mind searching for what he would say.

One minute late, the Panama Limited, up from New Orleans, came to a stop at Central Station in Chicago. Aaron Silverstein stepped out onto Michigan Avenue. He turned his face to a chill wind from the lake and found a few unruly April snowflakes on his shoulder. He hailed down a taxi and checked into a hotel on the Near West Side, the familiar Jewish neighborhood. He planned to spend the afternoon on the telephone, looking people up.

And searching for something to say.

His room was warm. He loosened the collar. Stood at the window and stretched his muscles. So much to do this week. All of it important. And outside the window he saw Chicago. Chicago pulsating with all the energy the twentieth century had to offer. His Chicago. He was home.

Around ten on Wednesday he took a cab to the Loop where Terry O'Shaughnessy practiced law. In law school he had trapped Terry in an argument and had smothered him with it. The two had been friends since. Terry litigated now. He defended railroads accused of avaricious tariffs and meatpackers accused of slack weights in barrels. He dressed in boardroom suits and had a paneled office that looked out over Lake Michigan.

○ ○ ○

"Let's face it," he explained to Aaron Silverstein, "courts know avarice when they see it. Who am I to think they don't. The best thing to do is put a polite face on it. Nice crookedness keeps the country running. Courts understand that. "The topic turned to the coming White Sox trial. Aaron and Terry always held season's tickets together.

"What will happen?" Aaron Silverstein asked.

"Over," said O'Shaughnessy.

"Some deal?" asked Silverstein.

"Nothing like that," Terry answered. "But all eight players will walk away and so will the five gamblers. "Care to know why?"

"I don't waste money on railroad tickets."

"All right." O'Shaughnessy tilted back and put his legs on the desk. "Cook County has a new prosecutor, George Crowe. He will prosecute."

"I remember him. He prosecuted in the Bobby Frank murder."

"Yes. Now three of the players, Eddie Cicotte, Joe Jackson and Lefty Williams, signed statements that amounted to confessions and for that they received immunity from prosecution."

"Nothing extraordinary."

"Well, when Crowe took over office a few months ago he found that all the statements and the waivers had disappeared from the prosecutor's office. They could not be found."

"Had what!"

"Disappeared. Gone. Vanished. Stolen. Now where is the state's case?"

"It's gone, too."

"Right. The defense will ask for them and the state will not be able to produce them. The state will probably be laughed out of court. The problem is it's anticlimactic. The new Commissioner, Landis, has banned the eight from baseball forever no matter what the court does. He's ruined the White Sox."

"Who did it?"

"Who knows? Comiskey? Your gambler friend Rothstein:? Does anyone know?"

"Can Comiskey rebuild the White Sox?"

"It will be years. If ever. Why he was so stingy with the best players in the game is anyone's guess. He even made them wash their own uniforms. Talented men who only wanted to be paid what they were worth."

"Men on pedestals, but with feet of clay."

"Idolized by a country too idealistic for its own good. Can't expect crookedness. Can never see where it's headed. Seems that we're always a generation behind in greatness. But how about it? Do you ever see talent where you are? A Christy Matthewson to send to the White Sox?"

"I can send you the next Christy Matthewson. He pitches in his long red underwear."

"If a man called 'Shoeless Joe Jackson' can be the best hitter in baseball, why can't the best pitcher pitch in his Long Johns?"

"I think I will simply leave him for Mister Comiskey to find on his own. The White Sox are Mister Comiskey's little red wagon. Us? Our job is just to pay our way in. I'll buy your ticket for the opener."

Now came the hard part.

Wednesdays his mother attended a club meeting that began at noon and lasted most of the afternoon. His father would be at home alone.

Around twelve-thirty the taxi dropped him in the suburbs in front of the neat two story home his father had built after he became successful. He knocked at the door of the house where he grew up.

The slight man with silver hair who answered frowned slightly then nodded and turned back down the hall. In the kitchen he put water into a tea kettle and brought out two teacups. He and Aaron sat, saying nothing to one another. Neither, as the kettle whistled, seemed to have much to say. After a little talk, Aaron raised the subject.

"I plan…that is, I hope, to marry," he said.

O O O

"Wonderful," said his father, brightening, "you will be happy. She knows?"

"No. Not yet. Father, it's outside the faith."

"Outside. Oh," said his father. The bright expression turned vacant and then thoughtful as he stirred the tea. 'And you wish me to tell your mother? She is not here. This is Wednesday. Can you tell me about her?"

And so for almost an hour he spoke to his father, surprised that he was saying things that he had never said to any person, about meeting her, talking to her and having deep, unexplainable, mysterious feelings toward her.

"This feeling," said his father, "will it die? Sometimes it is best if a feeling of romance or love simply goes away with time."

"No. No it won't. I don't want it to."

"Yes. Yes, it won't. This news will kill your mother, you know."

"I have hoped that it will not."

"And how will you support her?"

"The stores."

"The stores. And something is about those stores."

"They do well."

His father was silent for a full minute. "Something about those stores," he said then resumed the silence. Stirring, again perhaps to seek something in his teacup he said "although it may kill your mother, it may not. If I tell her that Justice Brandeis married outside the faith and that was all right with President Wilson, then perhaps it may not kill her. That is what I will do."

"Thank you. But I have another problem."

"It is?"

"It is that I do not know how to carry on a courtship. I do not know what to do."

His father laughed. "Courtship. Ha! Romance. Ha! I scoff at those. They are simple. I met your mother coming over on the boat, you know?"

O O O

"Virtually a legend."

"When I decided to marry your mother I sent my brother David to her and he said 'Clara, Moshe Silverstein wishes to marry you'."

"I have no brother."

"Yes," said his father, "well, it was an example. But you are a lawyer, and brilliant, can you not draw up a contract proposing marriage, saying 'Aaron Silverstein will do this and that and Miss So-and-so…'"

"Miss Hearn. Her name is Miss Hearn."

"…and that Miss Hearn will do thus and such?"

"That is not customary down there."

"Then would you like for me to go down there and say to Miss…"

"Hearn."

"Say to Miss Hearn, 'Aaron Silverstein wishes to marry you'?"

"That would be only a very last resort."

"But you are creative. You will find a way."

"I suppose I must."

Moshe Silverstein thumped the table. "There you are. If you must, then you will. It is foreordained. There is nothing left to discuss."

Moshe gathered up the teacups.

"Aaron," his father said as they walked down the hallway, "since you graduated from law school have you taken a single, solitary case?"

"I do not believe so."

"When I tell your mother, may I tell her you will take up the practice of law?"

"Tell her I will in a year or two, yes."

"Aaron, do you know sacrifice?"

"I don't know."

"No, no you don't. You didn't come here. I did."

"You haven't made me need it."

"A law school is sacrifice."

Aaron said nothing. He stood on the steps.

"I will tell your mother, Aaron. She will be happy for you."

"Yes," said Aaron.

"I love you, Aaron," said his father and he closed the door.

Aaron walked to the corner and took a trolley to town.

○ ○ ○

As he packed the idea hit him. He had a way to satisfy his friend's request for automobiles and to carry out his courtship with Miss Hearn. But it was after eight and he had to retrace his steps from yesterday to the Sears Roebuck warehouses and to talk to his purchasing agent again. Then he had to be back at Central Station by eleven-thirty to catch the Panama Limited south.

"Baseball uniforms," he told the supervisor he jokingly referred to as his "purchasing agent".

"Any color?"

"Red, white and blue."

Sporting good had its own section in the huge building and the two rummaged among boxes. "Why red, white and blue?" asked the agent.

"I'm going to sponsor a baseball team."

Silverstein looked at his watch. He had to give himself at least half an hour to get to the station.

"I think you're going to owe me season tickets," said the agent. They opened more boxes. The agent held up a jersey. "Look at this."

Silverstein unfolded a white flannel jersey. *Mamma mia,* he said softly.

In his hand he held the top half of a baseball uniform in a soft wool flannel that was white, but not quite white. It was a soft cream, or ivory color and was so light in weight a player could stand beneath the summer sun and still feel cool. At the sleeves and along the buttons ran a trim of navy blue. "Numbers," said Silverstein, "some of the teams are going to them."

"These caps," said the agent, pulling one from a box. "Beautiful." He put it on. "Batter up," he said.

'Strike three. You're out," said Silverstein.

"They're going to a team in California called 'the Culver City Diablos'," said the agent. The jerseys had the letters CCD embroidered in red letters with a red pitchfork running through the "D".

"That can come off," said Silverstein.

Every uniform had a pair of nubby woolen stockings in navy blue. The knickers were spare and trim to the knee to emphasize the athletic form of the player and each pair of knickers had a belt of black leather. The blue-trimmed high straight collars closed at the throat by means of a heavy brass safety pin and someone had obviously spared no expense outfitting the Culver City Diablos.

"They make the movies out there. They're rolling in it," said the manager.

"How much for these?" asked Silverstein.

"Buck a uniform," said Silverstein's purchasing agent. "They'll go to your warehouse tonight. God loves us, I know this. We're sharing in the fortunes of the tinsel Mecca."

"God helps those who help themselves," Silverstein said.

"He helps those who help themselves to the movie fortunes. So that's why we're helping ourselves to some baseball uniforms," said the agent. Aaron Silverstein smiled and agreed. "Someone down there tells me I should smile more," said Silverstein.

"Could be right," said the purchasing agent.

His last day in Chicago he spent with an old gambling associate. His friend had established some new ties with the growing bootleg trade and the bootleg industry depended upon automobiles. They never had enough because soo many were taken by police or shot to pieces.

○ ○ ○

In Meridian Aaron Silverstein remained awake for two nights removing pitchforks from baseball jerseys. The next morning he wrote a check for five hundred dollars to open a bank account and he packed the uniforms in the back of his car.

The morning after that he drove straight to the insurance office of Win Harrigan. Today with the help of the uniforms and the money he planned to put his plan of courtship into motion. And in addition he had a new business proposal to put before Win Harrigan.

○ ○ ○

"He said what?" asked Win Harrigan a second time.

"He asked if we could supply up to five serviceable automobiles," Silverstein replied. "Can we?"

"A few, at least," said Win Harrigan. "Five is a lot. For how much?"

"Seven to eight hundred each, depending."

"And how much does a new Model T Ford sell for?"

"About eight hundred.

"So we would make as much as Henry Ford gets for a new one and we don't have to make it."

"Just steal it."

"My friend buys all he can from dealers," Silverstein said. "But they have their other customers, too. Prohibition has made illicit liquor a big industry, and the industry is expanding. More and more deliveries to make. Every day, new places."

"It will have to be out of town games. We can't steal our own cars."

"What do we do with them after we steal them?"

"Deliver them to me."

"And you?"

"Put them in a crate and put them on the railroad to Chicago. I get a check in a few days and your share goes into your bank account. The team's account I should say. It will all look like the team's share of gate receipts and so forth. Since I'm going to sponsor the team it will just look like that's what I'm spending to be the sponsor."

Win Harrigan had opened every box. Beautiful baseball uniforms, stockings, jerseys, pants, lay across desks and chairs. The office had the look of the city bandstand on the Fourth of July, decked out in red, white and blue.

Win Harrrigan picked up the jersey and turned it to the number "one" on the back. "Manager's number," he said.

"Number one," agreed Aaron Silverstein.

"You know, I've always dreamed. Dreamed that this would be a big team. Go into a league." He looked away from Aaron Silverstein. The voice became distant and reflective. "But it's been hard. Finding players. Persuading people to play. I don't do it for me."

"No."

"I do it for roads. To convince the state. It proves that we need roads in this part of the state. To bring people in. Roads bring development."

"But you can't take cars yourself. You'll have to have an…ah…an associate."

"I have a man who can do it. He hires out as a tractor driver but it's not full time work. He can get the cars to you. He's the sort who would walk back and sleep on the side of the road for two days. Twenty dollars. For the money, he'd clam up. I could spare him since I hardly play him."

Ten minutes later Aaron Silverstein and Win Harrigan appeared together at the State Bank of Clarke. Aaron Silverstein opened an account for the team with five hundred dollars.

The Clarke County Democrats took on the name "George Washington's All American Stores Clarke County Democrats," although people never did use that long name. And in Culver City, California, the Diablos played the season in uniforms hastily made from the boxes they received from Sears Roebuck in Chicago, of taffeta bedspreads.

ELEVEN

NEWS THAT THE DEPARTMENT STORE chain now sponsored the Democrats brought an electric response from the town.

"Roads!" touted the booster committee. "'Roads will come.' 'Montgomery, pay attention!'". Miss Hearn even brought their United States Congressman into the act.

"Dear Congressman," she wrote.

"George Washington's All American Stores, the famous chain, has decided to sponsor the Clarke County Democrats, the pride of this section of our state. One of their wishes is to have a mural painted on the fence depicting The Father of Our Country. Would you please send us several different likenesses and/or scenes of our Country's father for our guidance? With thanks. Sincerely, Amy Hearn (Miss) State Bank of Clarke for the business manager."

Nine days later a package arrived special delivery. Tomorrow she would embark on a grand project

From the likenesses the Congressman sent Miss Hearn studied the Father of the Country in various depictions. She rejected the one of George Washington kneeling beneath a tree, praying that winter at Valley Forge and she rejected Washington seated in a chair holding a sword and surrounded by books and Washington standing in a stiff pose gesturing with his right hand as if calling strike two on the outside corner..

The scene she settled on would span twenty or more feet across the fence from left center field to almost dead center. It would be Emanuel Gottlieb Leutze's 1851 depiction of Washington crossing the Delaware River on Christmas morning, 1775.

There stood Washington against a bright sky, a foot propped on the thwart of the boat, his eyes fixed on the far shore. His brave men seated around him struggled against blocks of ice and pulled at their oars. No other baseball field—not in Alabama nor anywhere else could, or would--match such a scene. *Hooray for us! Signal! Signal!* she thought.

Putting the idea before William Harold the Third and Mister Harrigan she added that the Delaware mural would have an added psychological effect. The sight of men struggling against a frozen river would have a cooling effect on patrons in the seats on a hot summer day. Mister Harold and Mister Harrigan pursed their lips and locked their eyes, but they assented.

Next, as far as Win Harrigan was concerned, was the advertising program. By way of a flyer he brought together the team and the booster committee for a joint meeting at the ballfield. Standing before the bleachers he distributed the red, white and blue uniforms. Next he outlined the "hit it over me and win" program and asked the boosters to promote it around town. Signs painted on the fence would advertise a business and say "hit it over me and win...something." His Harrigan Insurance Agency would buy the first sign, in left field, and would say *"hit it over me and win $15.00. The Harrigan Agency. Insurance."*

Finally came the announcement of the "Washington Crossing the Delaware" mural, to be paid for out of team funds. To be ready for opening day on May 13 he stated that a professional sign painter would be engaged right away.

Fingers raised a hand. "I think I can do that," he said.

"You?" asked Win Harrigan. "You can paint a mural?"

Fingers repeated that he could if he had the paint and supplies and then if he did have the paint and supplies, the mural would certainly be complete by opening day.

Fingers did give everyone the impression that he was "artistic". He taught piano to young boys in the town, for some reason only to boys, in his home, not to girls. Mister Shaw, the first baseman, principal at the Institute did not send his son to learn piano. He did not say why. No one objected to Fingers' proposal. On Monday Mister Harold would open a charge account at the hardware store for Fingers' use.

Win Harrigan's "Hit It Over Me" program took William Harold the Third somewhat by surprise. He did not know about Win Harrigan's idea. The bank, he knew, should buy a sign. But he did not know how his great-uncle Francis X. Harold would react to simply giving somebody ten or fifteen dollars just for hitting a home run. William Harold the Third evaluated his services to the Democrats. The services, after all, came from the bank, not necessarily from him. In conclusion, he decided that the bank had been generous. The bank would buy a sign, but it would be as close to the right field foul pole as possible.

Everyone on the Democrats hit right-handed with two exceptions, Cousins and Richie. Cousins was a classic left-handed hitter, lean, with an affection for low, inside pitches. He hit a lot of singles and doubles, but nothing that really carried. Richie had almost no power at all. Cobb hit cross-handed and Win Harrigan could not break him of it, so he did not know how to classify Cobb. William Harold ordered the bank's sign painted about ten feet inside the right field foul pole to forestall criticism and it read "Hit it over me and Win $10.00. *State Bank of Clarke County*". He hoped for the best, which was that no one would hit it over the sign.

Aaron Silverstein sent word from Meridian that the baseball field ought to have a flagpole and a flag and in fact he had already ordered one from Chicago. It would be delivered by Railway Express consigned to the State Bank of Clarke County. It did in fact arrive on a big green truck the day after Aaron Silverstein's telegram arrived. Miss Hearn signed the delivery receipt.

○ ○ ○

Theodosia Gordon chose something from the store's summer line to wear to the game. It was expected that she, as head seamstress and floor manager of George Washington's All-American Stores, would be there. And Mister Silverstein had such good taste. Any woman would feel presentable and confident in the George Washington's dresses.

Now, with the game a week away, she and Eloise McCord sat in the Gordon living room and attempted to persuade Thornton Gordon to attend also and Thornton could not make himself say yes.

"I just can't be with those people…" he pleaded to the pair. "Not yet."

"Of course you can, Thornton," said Theodosia.

Thornton shook his head. "Can't you see all those people looking at me?"

"And I know they won't," said Eloise. "They will be looking at the game and they will be glad to see *you.*"

"I think you should go, Thornton," said Theodosia and Thornton attempted to bury himself in his chair.

"If I think about it I suppose I have no reason not to go," he finally said. "And I suppose I am no different from so many others. Things just piled up, didn't they?"

"They did," said Eloise. "Thornton, we all lost Edward. And I know you should go."

$$O \; O \; O$$

William Harold the Third had his own decisions to make and he would, as far as he could, manipulate history.

When he made the original schedule he arranged the opening game to be against a rather tough team that played out of Selma. But with the sponsorship developments and the first-class uniforms community pride came into play. The power of boosting and where boosting would take the town came into play. He felt that it was important for the Democrats to bring in a win to open the season; a loss might have a deflating effect.

In an afternoon on the long distance telephone the moved the game with the Selma team to an open date in August and arranged a game with a fraternal lodge team from Mobile, who were happy to have the money William Harold offered.

The team had the nickname "the Alcoholics," used laughingly, and no one had ever seen the Alcoholics play a game sober and no one knew if they had any other name. No one had ever seen them win a game, either.

Miss Hearn caught on. "Are you cheating the patrons, Mister Harold?" she asked.

William Harold the Third became brusque. "Someday you may become a business manager, Miss Hearn," he said. "It's not just a man's domain. Look at the strides we have made for 1921. Our pitcher is back, having settled some differences at home I believe, whatever they were, may they never be mentioned again, although I never thought him to be vital. Judge us not by the flaws of our opponents but by our pure heartedness. By the purity of well-played sport. We offer our patrons the purity of sport. There is no cheating about it." A few minutes later Miss Hearn handed William Harold the Third the figures he would need for his next meeting with his great-uncle.

○ ○ ○

And at the field Fingers worked harder and harder and more hurriedly. He made countless trips to the hardware, taking the picture of Washington Crossing the Delaware with him. He and the owner spent time matching paints to the colors in the painting, the grays of the ice, the patriotic red, white and blue of the flag, the chill dawn. Also, he purchased twenty feet of canvas tarpaulin. This he erected on poles about six or eight feet in front of the fence and he worked invisibly behind it. If people, he explained, could see the work as it progressed, the drama of the unveiling would be destroyed. People agreed.

At last, thought William Harold the Third. When Win Harrigan approached him three years ago with the idea of a baseball team, he expressed some doubts. Frankly, Win Harrigan told William Harold the Third, he himself had some doubts. But he worked hard, huckstered, cajoled and found players. *Like a true booster he had crowned the effort by purchasing a surplus bus.*

Now, in thirty minutes, the 1921 season would begin. Yesterday, just before six, Aaron Silverstein arrived from Meridian. William Harold the Third had waited for him in a chair in what amounted to the lobby of the hotel over the drugstore. Today the Sponsor sat in what amounted to a section of the stands roped off for important people. He watched batting practice and infield practice and asked why the opponents had the name Alcoholics.

William Harold the Third, Aaron Silverstein, Miss Hearn and the mayor watched as a troop of Boy Scouts escorted the new flag to the new flagpole, raised it and saluted it. Win Harrigan made his team stand respectfully near home plate.

The moment had now arrived to unveil the mural.

Win Harrigan gathered up the booster committee. The occupants of the box joined them. They would all proceed to center field for the unveiling.

As a courtesy Win Harrigan invited the manager of the Alcoholics to join the group and they crossed the infield and crossed the outfield to the place where Fingers stood beside the tarpaulin. In a moment they would see Fingers' twenty foot depiction of Emanuel Gottlieb Leutze's stirring creation, the heroic Washington crossing the icy river.

At a signal from Win Harrigan Fingers pulled the rope releasing the tarpaulin.

Miss Hearn said the first words: "Fingers, you've made George Washington into a midget," she said, aghast. And it was true. While most of the figures in the boat were nearly life-size, the figure of George Washington was only about three feet tall.

"I had to," said Fingers. "I didn't have room at the top."

Some of the booster committee began to frame the picture with their hands moving this way and that thinking that perhaps they were seeing some sort of optical illusion. The manager of the Alcoholics giggled, waved to Washington and said "hey, Shorty." That was too much for Miss Hearn. She turned and stalked away toward the stands. On the way she kicked second base and did a little one-legged jig holding her foot.

No one enjoyed the game more than Thornton Gordon. Once or twice he stood and clapped and called out "huzzah" or even "yippee." Friends who he had not seen in a long time climbed to the Gordons' seats and shook his hand. Theodosia saw the Thornton she had not seen in a long time. *I'll try to get him to all the games,* Theodosia thought. *It will put some color back in his face.*

The game ended in a 22 to zero score, which satisfied William Harold the Third. As the patrons left Eloise McCord said to Theodosia "would you and Thornton come with me?"

They walked out along the left field line to the base of the flagpole. She said "this was shown to me. No one knows who paid for it or who put it here. But I think it belongs here." Theodosia read the bronze tablet and covered her face with her hands. Thornton placed his arms around her. "Someone..." was all he said. He tightened his arms around Theodosia. "Someone...." The polished bronze letters read

"In Memory of private Edward Thornton Gordon
United States Expeditionary Force
France – 1918."

TWELVE

Even though the Meridian Firehouse team bragged more than anyone could stand, and made people avoid them if possible, and told people what heroes they were they still brought the city an element of pride. Some of the firemen had played in the now defunct Cotton States League; and had got their jobs for that reason. They thought themselves ballplayers first and firemen after that. If they lost a house to a fire, they dared any recrimination. Ball playing held a place above firefighting for the Meridian Firehouse team. The town ought to be aware of that.

Tree had played in the Cotton States League and now he burned with humiliation and he went around town fomenting a cry for revenge. The problem was that even if another game could possibly be scheduled with the Clarke County Democrats, the game would have to be played on the Democrats' field; the agreement between the teams specified home and home. Around town, people agreed the Democrats had to come to Meridian again so they could be brought down on the same field where they had triumphed.

Only one answer remained.

Meridian took pride as the commercial capital of half the state. Its rail yards clanked and groaned day and night with the sounds of switching and coupling and uncoupling, huffs and chuffs, and the long consists finally shaking off their indolence, gathering their energies in prolonged noises and finally bidding the city summary farewell.

Meridian had been shown up. Too big for its britches. Fallen from the Cotton States League into obscurity. And the city's mayor saw the crisis of civic pride and he had to put an end to it. On a sheet of paper he noted his arguments. He noted the favors he had granted; incidents he had overlooked; the promises yet to be fulfilled; the threats he could make. "Connect me to the M&O," he told his secretary.

Across town at the Mobile & Ohio Rail Road's office, E. C. Carswell, the General Agent, hung up the phone and pulled himself out of his chair. He walked out of his office and asked his secretary "has that letter to the Crescent City Stevedores gone?"

"It will today," the lady replied. "It's in the mail room".

"Pull it back. Pull it back," Carswell said. "For God's sake, right now."

When the letter originally intended for the Crescent City Stevedores in New Orleans arrived instead in Thomasville addressed to the Clarke County Democrats it brought William Harold the Third to his feet with a whoop. Without his coat he left the bank at a near run, his destination the office of Win Harrigan.

The two looked over the contents with glee. Somehow the United States Postal Service had delivered pure gold. To their estimation, it had delivered about eight thousand dollars of pure gold.

Warm, unstirring, bleached by moonlight, Tallahatta might have been an old tintype, a picture found in an album, a landscape of forest and field brought out at night in wispish grays falling away from silvered whites,

98

only as shadows, that traced themselves toward distant, smoky blacks, a poetic Tallahatta that time could never alter, an image of primitive earth that captured their minds and made them one, and drew them into its shadows, a place from where they could never return, and held them still, each of them barely conscious of the other's presence but linked by their thoughts and the occasional touch of a hand or the rustle of a piece of clothing.

Leonard would have let the night go on and on. But he had to get an answer to this question. Leonard wanted to talk about the team's invitation to play in the M&O series. The last game would be played on Sunday. Even though Frances had conceded the Sunday games idea, Leonard wanted to make sure.

"Jesus don't give a hoot about baseball." An awkward way to start, but he thought it was his strongest point.

"You told me that."

"Know what else Jesus don't give a hoot about?"

"What?'

"Jesus don't give a hoot 'bout dancin' either. You know what?"

"What?"

"They got a music store in Meridian."

"And?"

"Well, it's got a music box. You know, a talking machine. Victrolas they call them.

"Are you talking about baseball or are you talking about talking machines?"

"Well, they played a song out it for me."

"You done told me about it."

"I'll sing it. We'll dance."

"Dance to the song?"

"Watch. Hold out your arms. Wait. Let me wind up the machine."

Leonard wound the imaginary machine with a cranking motion, then sang:

I will gather stars out of the blue
For you. For you.
I'll make a string of pearls out of the dew
For you. For you.
Over the highway and over the street
Carpets of clover I'll lay at your feet.
There is nothing in the world I wouldn't do
For you. For you.

"Leonard!"

"That's how the song goes. You can't gather stars. I know that."

"But your singing is bad. It's awful". She giggled and tried to imitate Leonard.

"See how bad it is?"

"Well, you see what it's like with a talking machine. That's what a talking machine sounds like."

"Then I don't want one," and Frances began to laugh.

"I do. Dance with me again?"

"Leonard, you sing awful. You dance awful, too. Leonard, we almost fell off the porch."

"Just once." Leonard gathered Frances into his arms.

"I will gather stars…"

"Leonard, you're bad. Watch out!"

"Now a rag." Leonard flung out a leg. Then the other leg. The floor of the porch moaned and made a cracking sound.

"See?" yelped Frances.

"I know. But it's a whole world out there, Frances. Talking machines. Victrolas, and all those things."

"But this is West Alabama, Leonard. It's going to be like this forever in west Alabama."

"No it ain't. Not for you. Not for me."

"Leonard, I have my world. Just take me in your arms, Leonard Cassity. And you don't have to dance or sing or give me a talking machine. I have all the world I need."

○ ○ ○

Foster Hawkins fumbled in his pocket for a dime to tip the Western Union boy. The boy touched a knuckle to the brim of his cap and pedaled away. Foster Hawkins opened the brown envelope and took out the telegram. It read

"Expect Ludgood Williamson this club arrive Meridian July 28. Stop. Make reservations good hotel duration of series. Stop. Purchase grandstand tickets length of series third row behind visitor dugout. Stop. S/Comiskey"

Foster Hawkins could think of no one with the name Ludgood Williamson associated with the Chicago White Sox baseball club.

○ ○ ○

Faithful to the instructions Foster Hawkins stood at the platform of the Alabama and Vicksburg depot on Thursday. His problem was that he did not know how he would recognize a "Ludgood Williamson". He did not know how he would recognize him nor what he would do with him afterward.

The car from Jackson discharged a half dozen or so passengers. Not a big crowd yet for the series, Hawkins thought. But there would be an excursion train later. Hawkins recognized the man with the carpetbag. He was a salesman who called on the printing companies. Two ladies with hatboxes and a male companion apparently were expected by another man who hurried forward and the group exchanged kisses and handshakes. Some wedding or something Hawkins thought.. He studied the last man to step from the car. The man wore a large dark brown fedora with a partridge feather in the band and he carried a large, worn valise or briefcase with leather straps. He had pulled the fedora low on his forehead. Something about that briefcase Hawkins thought. He had seen it. At spring training. Many times.

"Mister C…." Hawkins said, stepping forward.

"Williamson," interrupted the man. "Get me to the hotel. Where am I staying?"

"Stockmen's Hotel, sir," Hawkins answered. "It's where all the cattle buyers stay. First class." The two walked to Hawkins automobile.

Williamson settled into the passenger's seat with the valise in his lap. "What are we looking at here, Hawkins?" he asked in a peremptory tone.

"Name is Cassity. Twenty-one or twenty-two. Very good and natural. May have some control problems early. Still strong in the late innings. Plenty of velocity on the fastball, tight curve. He can't jump right now. But in a year…."

"God damn Cicotte and Williams," said Williamson. "Couple of ingrates."

Hawkins added, "from what I hear, his honesty is a strong point. He's a sincere young man. Married. Has a brand new baby."

"Good. Glad you sent me that letter. Well, sent Comiskey that letter. But by the way, about that letter…"

"Sir?"

"It said something about the 'lively ball' or something like that. We don't mention it."

"But…"

"It's the same ball you played with in 1911. Cork center. Just the same."

"But last year Ruth hit fifty nine home runs and this year he already has over thirty. Is there an explanation?"

"It just happened, that's all. Just happened." With that, conversation ended until Ludgood Williamson arrived at Stockmen's Hotel and told Hawkins to pick him up an hour before tomorrow's game.

○ ○ ○

Win Harrigan spent an hour Friday morning in his room alone, mulling over today's lineup card. His only decision was whether to start Bonehead Arceneaux or Richie in center field. Bonehead seemed less likely to feel pressure because Bonehead never felt pressure; Richie did not hit quite as well, but Richie could bunt and had speed... He chose Richie; he planned to make Richie bunt, even with two strikes, hoping for one or two early runs. Leonard of course had to hold this big team in check. He had doubts about the second game. He had no real starter. He believed Leonard could win the first game, and if he stayed strong could also win the third. That was a lot to stake on one pitcher but he felt it was his best, maybe his only, choice.

Leonard could win two games, he believed that. He had to. He told himself that and then he descended to the lobby.

Most of the Democrats had already gathered to wait for Win Harrigan to bus them to the stadium even though that was an hour away, and he admitted to himself that they looked sharp in their new uniforms. He had instructed the team to launder and press them and he had specifically warned Cobb not to spit into his crotch. Cobb stood with his back to Win Harrigan poking a finger into Richie's chest.

"Cobb." Buckles who did not like Cobb walked past him.

"Yeah?"

"Saw your old lady here last night."

Win Harrigan had isolated the team.

"Yeah?"

"She was with somebody."

Win Harrigan thought he saw telltale brown in the crotch.

"You chewing?" he asked. "I'll fine you ten dollars if I see tobacco juice down there. And hasn't that old woman of yours already told you she gets everything off this?" Cobb swallowed something. "But I ain't."

He found Constable, Leonard's roommate.

"How's Leonard?"

Constable gave a half-shrug. "Don't know. That is, I can't say. He's drawn in. Stale or something. Doesn't have an edge. I just don't think he's interested. Not even the usual bellyache. He was on his knees last night at bedtime."

"Maybe he's different from the religion."

"More religion than he needs."

"Nobody tells him how to use it.."

"Watch him."

So Win Harrigan crossed the lobby to Leonard.

"How's belly?" he asked.

"Fine," said Leonard.

"Nothing?"

"No."

Nobody talked to Leonard as he sat quietly at the back of the bus. Constable sat where he customarily set, in front behind Win Harrigan. Where William Harold the Third ordinarily sat Bonehead Arceneaux had moved up and babbled giddily. "Shut up," Win Harrigan told him. "Think about hitting with two outs and runners on second and third. Just shut up." He didn't want the team to feel tense, bottled up. But Bonehead was just too much. He looked at Questionable, two rows back, who looked absently out the window. Can't read him, he thought. Nobody could.

And that no one spoke to Leonard suited Leonard.

Frances had carefully laundered his uniform and scrubbed away every little stain. Some red clay at the right hip where he had slid into third in the May 8 game. Some green grass at the knee that came from stumbling in the infield when he muffed a bunt the game after that. To him they were just little insignificant badges of play that he didn't care about. But Frances had laundered them away, taken them away and made him brand new.

He thought. But he couldn't make himself think about baseball. Something came to him last night. *When I've done right by her, I'll feel better.* Something would tell him when that was. *Jesus don't give a hoot about baseball.* He knew that. *But he sure don't give a hoot about me either. So if Jesus don't give a hoot about it, then me neither.* That was what came to him last night. He wanted to tell Frances he would stay quit. But then she relented. *But why was she so happy just as she was? Why was it so important to her, that she was happy as she was? How could he love her so much?*

With the money from ball he could buy Frances a Victrola. With this money he could raise Frances to his mother's standards. Mister Harrigan promised him twenty-five dollars for a win. Five weeks pay at the sawmill.

Leonard had matured now. He was comfortable; his long, angular legs had the whole bench. He looked at his toes.

A year ago the strangers from Mississippi who gathered around the bus to look at the young man who threw the no-hitter would have seen a one-hundred-and-fifty-five pound youth disembark. In 1920 but now it was 1921. Now twenty-one and nearly twenty-two years old they saw no boyish figure. They saw a young man now at full growth, a man six feet one inches tall who weighed a little over one-hundred-and-sixty-five pounds. A young man made muscular and supple by Frances' cooking, by the days of wrestling to move pine logs, the nights of early bedtimes in a house without electricity, bedtimes that brought almost nightly lovemaking, making their lungs fill with the pure, cool night air of Tallahatta. Those nights he cradled her on his shoulder and Frances cried tears of joy and he would smooth away the tears, and then feel her fall asleep and he would fall asleep himself.

He paid no attention to these people. His spikes clattered as he crossed the gravel and into the portal. He did not notice the odd, chill wind that seemed to follow him in.

An hour before game time now and Leonard tossed a ball lazily with two other players. For a moment he thought one of the players on the other bench was looking at him. So he thought he would show him something. He wound up and threw a fastball. Richie caught it but his glove was a fielder's glove not a catcher' mitt. "Ow, Leonard!" he said. Leonard mostly just watched the stands fill. About half the stadium was already occupied. The stands buzzed with spectators talking to spectators. Leonard thought the sound was like bees around a hive.

Win Harrigan seemed satisfied that Cobb was keeping his crotch fairly clean and he had cautioned Medicine Men about burning sticks in front of the dugout. But while he delivered his lineup card to the opposing manager at home plate, a small wisp of smoke began to rise where the empty sacks of gear had been thrown. Across the field the Stokers sat on their bench. They had finished batting practice and were in the middle of infield practice. They turned a smooth double play and zipped the ball around the diamond. Everything said they could play baseball but that seemed not to impress Leonard at all.

A man with a megaphone came through the stands announcing the starting lineups. When he came within a few feet of Ludgood Williamson, Williamson snatched the card away and said "let me see that." When the man with the megaphone made a move to object, Foster Hawkins simply said "wait a minute" and to the megaphone man, Ludgood Williamson did not seem like someone to argue with and Williamson copied names into a scorebook.

Williamson looked again at the Stoker pitcher's name. He knew that pitcher. Anderson, and he had pitched in the Tri-State League. Clarke Griffith had signed him and he had pitched a game or two for the Senators and then disappeared. He was too old for the Big Leagues now, but he was certainly going to make it rough for Leonard Cassity. A good test of his mettle, Williamson said to Foster Hawkins. "Anderson, remember him?" Hawkins said yes.

O O O

The first batter Leonard faced drove the ball over the left field fence. Questionable watched it sail over his head by ten feet. Constable stood with his hands on his hips in front of the plate and glared at Leonard. As the batter crossed home plate Constable cleared his throat then spat a slimy wad onto the hitter's shoes. Behind the mound Leonard fiddled with the webbing of his glove, untied and retied his shoes and avoided looking at Constable. The umpire delivered a new ball to Leonard and that gave Leonard something new to fiddle with. He scratched around at the seams with a fingernail. He cast an eye under the brim of his cap at Constable who by now had turned his back to Leonard and had put his mask on.

The second batter did nearly the same thing as the first, but a catch by Questionable crashing into the fence turned the long ball that was probably a triple into an out. Leonard had an out and though the score stood at three to one, two pitches had been hit hard, and so, in the bottom of the first, the lead didn't look safe.

But Win Harrigan had evidently done some clever managing and had put his strategy to work early. He wanted to unnerve the M&O Firebox Stokers and he took them by surprise.

Medicine Men, batting first, bunted the second pitch down the first base line. Anderson the Stoker pitcher, now a bit overweight and not quite as able to bend as in his Tri-State days, reached down, lost his hold on the ball then made a late throw to first base. Medicine Men crossed the bag safe.

With Medicine Men at first Medicine Men the second batter did exactly the same thing, except that the first baseman taking no chances with Anderson, rushed in. He fielded the bunt and then stood astraddle the base line waiting for Medicine Men to arrive. Four feet from the baseman Medicine Men simply stopped running and the two players stood facing each other, eye to eye. The first baseman took a step toward Medicine Men and Medicine Men took a step backward, in the direction of home plate. The baseman took another step. Medicine Men took another step. The baseman poked the ball at Medicine Men and said "fucking Indian."

Medicine Men did a little tap dance out of the way and said "fucking white man."

The baseman began to run, chasing Medicine Men down the base path in the direction of home plate. Medicine Men the runner at first watched the frustrated first baseman for a moment and then dashed to second. Finally the baseman reached Medicine Men who was now nearly at home plate and lunged at him to attempt a tag which Medicine Men adroitly dodged and began to run to first. The baseman turned and threw to first base, inaccurately, and the high throw rolled down the right field line. Medicine Men now at second ran to third on the error and Medicine Men rounded first and stood on second as the right fielder picked up the ball. The Democrats had two men in scoring position and the ball had never left the infield, except for the throwing error.

Questionable drove a triple into right field and tagged and scored a batter later on a high fly ball by Mister Shaw. The Democrats ended the top half of the first with a three to nothing lead.

In the bottom of the second Leonard gave up two consecutive singles. Between the first and the second hit Constable stepped in front of the plate and shouted "Quit daydreaming, Leonard". Medicine men helped Leonard by turning a double play and finally Leonard recorded his first strikeout. The score remained three to one after two.

On the bench Constable came and sat next to Leonard. "You all right?" he asked.

"Sure, Constable," said Leonard so Constable got up and left and went and sat next to Win Harrigan and reported that he did not think Leonard was all right. "He's daydreaming out there." Win Harrigan got up and left. When he came back, he shoved something at Constable.

So Leonard went out for the home third still leading three to one and seemed as unsettled as in the first two innings. At three balls and no strikes on the leadoff hitter Constable called time. He walked to the mound. "Leonard," he said in an exasperated voice. "See this?" Constable reached under his chest protector and took something out.

"What is it?"

"The Holy Bible. King James Version. I'm never without it."

"What are you doing?" called the umpire from home plate.

By now Medicine Men had joined the conference and then came Doctor Pearlington from third and Mister Shaw from first base. All the infield had gathered around Leonard and Constable and the Holy Bible. Constable placed the Bible behind his protector and Doctor Pearlington suggested "why don't you pitch to where the Bible is, Leonard? Constable can move it around."

"Play ball," said the umpire.

"You should do that, Leonard," said Medicine Men. "Because you know why?"

Leonard gave Medicine Men a puzzled look. "I don't know why," he said.

"Because Baseball King going to kill you next inning if you don't," said Medicine Men.

The third then became a more or less routine inning for Leonard. Two strikeouts and one groundout. Leonard seemed to have regained his form.

On the bench Constable again sat next to Win Harrigan.

"How did you settle him down?" Win Harrigan asked.

"I didn't," Constable said. "The Goddam Baseball King did."

By the middle of the fifth the Democrats had taken a nine to three lead, helped by a four-run fourth inning of consecutive doubles and singles from the middle of the lineup.

Aaron Silverstein spent more of his time swiveled in his seat observing two men three rows behind him than he did watching the game.

As the official sponsor of the George Washington's All American Stores Clarke County Democrats he had paid for a box with eight seats near the Democrats' dugout, only half of which were filled. William Harold the Third the business manager and Miss Hearn from the bank and the mayor of Thomasville sat in the box. In one of the seats Miss Hearn had placed the adding machine she had brought from the bank. Now, when the teams changed sides she and Mr. Harold left to meet with the business manager of the Firebox Stokers in a room under the stands to count out the Democrats' share of the gate.

To William Harold the Third it appeared that about seven thousand tickets had been sold at a dollar apiece and the Democrats would receive forty per cent. And that was just the first day of the three game series. If the third game sold out he believed the Democrats would take home more than eight thousand dollars. No one noticed, not the mayor nor Aaron Silverstein nor even Miss Hearn had noticed that a coat pocket was pulled slightly down by the weight of a small nickel-plated revolver.

Leonard had now struck out one in the first, two in the third, one in the fourth and fifth and was working on a second in the fifth. Aaron Silverstein thought he heard the fastball making that familiar rattlesnake sound, but even though he was too far away, he knew it was making it. The curve had that tantalizing break to it at the last instant. Leonard had gained command of this game.

With two in his party now departed he suggested to the mayor of Thomasville that he visit his counterpart in the home team's box and so the mayor shuffled his way through the stands to the home side.

He knew that face under the fedora. When the Democrats had the field the two men worked intently, writing notes into a scorebook. He had seen the face a thousand times in the newspapers, nearly that many at the White Sox' field.

He studied the two men. The old fox! That's why he's here. He's after that pitcher. After Leonard. Aaron Silverstein could imagine himself telling his friend Terry O'Shaughnessey of the day he outfoxed the fox, for giving Comiskey what he deserved for ruining the White Sox with his tightfistedness. He knew the feeling Adam Rothstein had when he fixed the Series. Control. Gambling isn't gambling if the gambler controls the outcome. Alone in his box he looked out over the green pasture dotted with men in white uniforms with an unexplainable feeling of peace in him, the Democrats, some too old to be playing baseball, but playing for reasons he could not guess. But no one ever admits he's too old to play the game. That was the illusion of it and the truth of it. That was why everyone was here, everyone.

Today he would outfox the fox. Alone, with the thought, no one around him, Aaron Silverstein smiled.

On the change of sides he caught Doctor Pearlington's attention and had him fetch Win Harrigan to the box. He came to the low fence. Aaron Silverstein leaned across. "I want Leonard on a contract today," he told Win Harrigan.

"What?" asked Win Harrigan.

"Leonard. I want you to put him on a contract with this club."

"We don't sign contracts with players."

"With this one. A hundred dollars a game win or lose. I'll do it in my office tonight. He can sign in the morning."

"Lot of money."

"We have it. I just want him tied down so he can't move."

"I planned to give him the day free tomorrow. Not even dress."

"All the better. Let him stay clear of the stadium. We'll sign him tomorrow night. I want him the property of the Clarke County Democrats."

Buckles came by gathering up equipment. "Buckles," said Win Harrigan.

"Yeah, boss?" Buckles knew it couldn't be much. He knew he'd never play in this series.

"Time for you to go drain your lizard."

"Drain my….Oh, yeah, I know what you mean. I'll go drain my lizard."

Win Harrigan winked at Silverstein and Silverstein winked back. Buckles left to find an automobile.

The four-run fourth seemed to take a burden off Win Harrigan. His step was stronger, his back more erect. He seemed to want to be visible, to primp in front of this hostile crowd so in the middle of the sixth he again walked over to Aaron Silverstein's box. He talked about the news clippings he would send to the people in Montgomery, to the people who would determine the course of roads, who governed the directions that roads took.

For an instant Silverstein's and Win Harrigan's eyes joined. "We are a pair, aren't we?" said Silverstein. "You, your roads. Me, my dark motives and my need to control."

"Well, the whole thing is an illusion," said Win Harrigan.

"The game?"

"The game."

"Is there anything about it that's truth?"

"Leonard out there."

"Leonard is the truth?"

"Leonard is the fast ball. And the fast ball puts the honesty in the game.. Leonard is the truth. He is as much truth as the game needs."

THIRTEEN

Leonard could feel that dissatisfaction inside him beginning to ebb away. Now that he had the money he could make all that go away. Win Harrigan not only gave him the twenty-five dollars last night, he also said he wanted to talk to him about more. The twenty-five was more than enough as he walked the four blocks to the music store.

Last night he stayed in his room and wouldn't talk to Constable. He took some of the hotel stationery and made the list of the records he planned to buy. Frances would like the romantic songs and he would want some of the rags.

"Hi, Leonard," said the girl. They knew him by now, and then she said "your picture's in the paper." There he was, standing in front of the visitor dugout with Constable. The newspaper reporter had posed the two, telling them he wanted "today's battery, the veteran catcher and the sensational young twirler." So they stood there like statues. The headline over the picture said "Democrats Hand Stokers a Loss Before Thousands." She boxed up the Victrola and told Leonard to be careful with the records. Leonard looked at the labels. He would have to shore up the porch.

Leonard couldn't remember when he didn't have to be up at dawn or before dawn and go to work. Or he had to play a game or had to practice. So as he walked the four blocks back to the hotel with the Victrola in its box, he realized he had gotten bored.

He sat in a chair in the lobby, self-conscious about it, and felt the boredom growing until the idea came to him that he ought to write his mother a letter. He could tell his mother about the Victrola and he knew this would elevate Frances in his mother's eyes and he decided he should add something about the game for his father since his father told him he knew some of that Mobile and Ohio Railroad crowd. He didn't need to go in, he'd simply ride the trolley out to the ballpark and absorb some of the excitement. The game was an hour off now, a good time to get a look at the crowd and put that in the letter.

Leonard like the streetcar, the grinding of the steel wheels on the rails, and the aroma of the electricity popping off the line overhead and the lurching and swaying of the car on the springs; it all reminded him of Mobile, even though that reminded him of his mother and that he lived under his mother's thumb. He swayed and lurched with the car, and felt the freedom of it; it added exhilaration, him now coming home with the first real thing for Frances that he had ever given her.

Off the streetcar Leonard relaxed and let himself be pulled and joggled along by the crowd. About fifty yards ahead he saw the ticket booth where a sign at the top said in big red letters "BASEBALL TODAY."

He had fun doing this because no one recognized him, probably since no one expected yesterday's winning pitcher to be in a crowd paying its way into the game.

A single gate couldn't handle the crowd so another had been opened down the left field line where some bleachers had been put up, and another down the right field line with a sign "colored" above it.

The whole thing looked to Leonard like a circus or a carnival or a county fair or a pageant. Why hadn't he bought a Kodak? He did not know everything would be so big out here.

In the ticket line three men grinning and joking passed around a flask and yesterday Leonard had heard some dull clanking coming from somewhere and he saw a group of about two dozen people shaking cowbells, so he walked over. People referred to the Okalona, Houston and Calhoun branch the "Okalona Horse and Cow," for all the livestock it carried, the man explained and so everybody from Okalona brought cowbells. A minute or two later a man holding up tickets approached Leonard and said "ticket, sir?" then looked closely at Leonard, saw who he was and walked away.

Some man had set up a stand a few yards away and had a camera on a tripod. "Have your picture taken with the world's longest steer horn," said his sign. "Fifty cents".

Leonard walked over. The man wore an engineer's cap.

"Eight feet two inches tip to tip. I'm a Frisco man. Saint Louis San Francisco. I collect. This is a rare horn. Been offered a thousand for it. A rare opportunity for you and you'll show this picture some day to your grandchildren." The man stopped talking and looked closely at Leonard. "Hey," he said, "I know you. You're the young twirler. Saw you pitch yesterday. No charge for you, young man. Stand by the horns." The man clicked the camera. "Come back tomorrow."

The man hailed Leonard again as he left.

"Hey, wait Do you want a good time? Go ride the carousel. Down there," he pointed and Leonard could see that it was very colorful. "And see the two goats? They're my favorites. Take a ride."

Leonard walked away and felt warmer. Why had he felt cold in the July sun? Not just cold at that stand, but if Leonard had noticed he would have seen that the man's feet had unusual shapes, divided in two at the toes. Cloven feet. The man who owned the divided feet smiled as he watched Leonard approach the carousel.

The two goats had large liquid black eyes that gazed from shaggy manes and beards and golden coats. The two had a bench between them and Leonard sat. The calliope began to play and the carousel began to go round. Now Leonard could begin to feel those large black eyes anchored on him, from either side. "Leonard," said the goat on his left. The music had become regular and calming. He was taking a pleasant ride.

"Leonard," said the goat again, "your sin is not that you play baseball. Your sin is that you do not do enough for Frances."

"I never told that to anybody," said Leonard. "Never said it. How can you know?"

"We know," said the goat "Look around you. Say what you see."

"Horses and things."

"No, not horses and things, Leonard. These are the condemned. Here is where your home is, Leonard. A pleasant ride to lure more souls to us."

"See the car, Leonard?" said the goat and moved his eyes. "Isn't it beautiful? Isn't that what you promised Frances, even though you never said it?"

Plainly the Model T Leonard saw stood out. It must have been painted and repainted and then polished to a glow. Yes, thought Leonard, this was the car he had promised.

"You know now, Leonard," said the first goat. "So go. You should go. You have to go to town now. To the drugstore." The large black eyes arrested Leonard and gave to the goat an irresistible appeal. No. He could not go home without the car. The plan that came to him was foolproof and he walked to the place where the trolley would take him back to town.

○ ○ ○

And that night Leonard had a nightmare, bringing him awake in a sweat.

The Holy Ghost in the form of a white dove engaged in violent combat with the two goats. The Holy Ghost, diving and swooping at the goats' black eyes then veering away to return to the attack, the two goats, rearing, erect, swatting with their hooves at the Holy Ghost, their eyes flaring. Sometimes the Holy Ghost became two doves, each attacking a goat.

Frances had told Leonard the story from Genesis of Cain and Able, that Cain slew Able and that God had made Cain a fugitive and had laid a mark on him, cloven feet, so "people would know not to kill him."

After she told him Leonard said "but it's not true."

"What's not true?" Frances asked.

"That."

"That what?"

"That a man has cloven hoof."

"But it is true. That's what the Bible says."

Leonard got out of bed and went into the bathroom and the lavatory. He held his head under the running water.

Constable came in and urinated and went back to bed without saying anything.

FIFTEEN

Tallahatta Springs, Alabama
August 2, 1921

Dear Mother Cassity

Guess what! Leonard come home driving a flivver Sunday night! He bought it from a man at the ball park over at Meridian. Yes I know he is playing baseball again but it allows us to have a few things. This year they upped his money first to $10.00 and now to $25.00 if he wins. We are going to Thomasville to buy groceries Friday after Leonard gets paid. It is wonderful!

Love Frances

YESTERDAY AT THE DRUGSTORE HE explained his problem. "Here," said the pharmacist, "this is used to unconstipate horses and cattle. A tablespoon ought to do you."

Now that Constable had dressed and gone downstairs Leonard looked at the tall glass bottle. "Syrup of Black Draught," it said in embossed letters along the side. A tablespoon said the pharmacist. The bottle held nine ounces.

Leonard uncorked the bottle and drank half. Then he poured the rest down the sink and threw the bottle away. It should be enough, he thought. As he stepped aboard the bus he could already feel his bowels begin to rumble.

And now with the game an hour old Leonard knew it wasn't going to be much longer. Still, he had done all he could. He had to help the team get a lead and they had one. He had struck out six.

Maybe it was wrong but he had to do it. He might control the rumbles one more batter and so he walked behind the mound and looked at his players, at Questionable in left, yesterday's pitcher, at Bonehead Arceneaux in center and Fingers in right; at the infield, Doctor Pearlington at third, Medicine Men at short and second and Mister Shaw, the Institute principal at first and at Constable. A long time ago he told Cobb he would go down there and strike them all out. His team now.

Now. Them? Or Frances.

When the next batter topped a ball and Leonard fielded it, the rush came, wet and warm down his pants. He made the throw to first and called to Constable.

Constable looked at the brown stains from the seat of Leonard's pants to his knees, down both legs. "Jesus, boy, you're a mess."

He waved an arm toward the bench. "Manager," he called.

SIXTEEN

Tallahatta Springs, Alabama
August 19, 1921

Dear Mother Cassity

Yesterday three men came by the house. They was the Clarke County Sheriff and two men said they was from the Mississippi bureau of theft. They wanted to know if we own a flivver. I said most certainly we do <u>not</u> own a flivver and they looked around the yard a little bit and said thank you ma'am and left. Soon as they left I put the baby in the stroller and hotfooted it to the sawmill to tell Leonard. He said I done the right thing and there wasn't nothing to it. To go home. But I want to tell you that ain't the kind of thing that happens every day. Baby fine other than some prickly heat.

Love Frances

SEVENTEEN

Tallahatta Springs, Alabama
September 9, 1921

Dear Mother Cassity

Yesterday the three men came back and arrested Leonard. Soon as they set foot on the property Leonard headed for the back door but the sheriff chased him around back. They took him to jail at Thomasville. Today I got Fergie to watch the baby and I walked to Thomasville. He says he bought the car but they got a colored man at Meridian says he saw Leonard crank the car and drive it off. Mother Cassity I have to believe Leonard. He is close with money and I know he had it. Mister Harrigan of the baseball team came by before me. Mr. Harrigan says the colored man needs to be lynched so he won't talk in court but they ain't got no reason to lynch him yet. They are working on it. Leonard says they got a law allows Leonard to be taken to Mississippi and put in jail and they will come for him on Monday or Tuesday to put him in Grove Hill so a judge can decide about that.

We love you, Frances

O O O

They came for Leonard on Saturday, the three men. The car came into sight around the little bend down the road and stopped under the oak at the front of the house.

Frances and Leonard had dressed to go to town and Frances had bathed and dressed Leonard, junior, and he smelled like baby powder, looking up out of his basket. In Thomasville they planned to spend their money. She needed shoes, Leonard, junior, everything.

Frances, at the front screen, saw the gold star on the door and saw three men get out, the younger man with the cane who had been here before, an older man and the Clarke County sheriff. Frances saw the piece of white paper on the sheriff's hand. What's gone wrong she thought. *Where?* "Leonard has to come with us," said the sheriff.

"He can't," Frances said, now holding tightly to the screen door. "We're busy." She heard Leonard inside, saying nothing and she heard the back door make a noise.

Why hadn't any of them told her something? The sheriff heard the back door, too, and ran. When he found Leonard Leonard had pressed himself to the wall behind the privy. The sheriff walked him in handcuffs to the oak tree and waited for the two men to join him from the porch. Frances saw Leonard's eyes, wide, wild, helpless. What had happened had happened so fast and no one had said why. All the doors slammed shut but only the sheriff looked back. He gave Frances an embarrassed glance and Frances stood on the porch with nothing to say and no one to say it to, wanting to run, but Tallahatta offered no place to run to. Tallahatta was what it always was and was going to be forever, the worst place in the world to be afraid, and Frances was alone in it.

So the afternoon wore on and Frances set herself up on the front porch in her rocking chair in the September heat and looked down the road, where it took the little bend. They would bring Leonard back. Nobody had told her why but pretty soon they would know it was wrong and Leonard would come back. Leonard, junior, stirred and cried once, and Frances, numb, sat and watched the sun go down, seeing only barely the green trees make their retreat into the darkness, pulling away, forgetting her, leaving her listless, devoid, a limp form in the night, letting her terror have its way with her.

○ ○ ○

No moon had risen no lamp was worth the effort. A milky shadow she walked through the blackened house. Men do cruel things to one another but now she had two things to do, one that she must look presentable when they brought Leonard back and the other that she must take care of Leonard, junior. How could she live out here, just she and him? She had to move them but then the disbelief of it returned. Her bath, her bath, that would come next and so she gave herself the favor of a kerosene lamp then stoked up the fire to heat her water. That gave her some time to mash some carrots and measure out some applesauce and hold the baby in her lap. Then she bathed.

She sat again on the porch. It wouldn't be long now. She had left the house for more water, looked up at the Milky Way.

One night when they were like this Leonard had said "Frances, you see the Milky Way?"

"Where, Leonard?" she replied.

"It's stars. It's a big white band of stars. So lay back and let your eyes adjust. It's a white stripe going that way. See?"

"Oh, yes, I see. It's beautiful."

"All that's just stars, you know."

"It's beautiful."

"Frances, would you like me to take you to the Milky Way?"

"How would you get us there?"

"In a Ford. In a Model T Ford."

"What would we do when we got there?"

"We'd just be us."

"Leonard, did you like the meat loaf tonight?"

"It was special."

"Leonard, and I'm going to call it 'Milky Way meatloaf' and only make it on special nights when we see the Milky Way."

If she made no sound herself the stillness overcame her and she felt the silence descend as a suffocating, extinguishing web.

Then around twelve as she lay in bed the beasts woke her up. She was fatigued, and in these few minutes she had drowsed; she had to stay awake for Leonard's return but the beasts woke her up. From her drowse she could hear them panting and prowling outside her window, making heavy, dark, open-mouthed breaths. She had to pull the covers over her head and lie very still. The wild hogs or the bears, ravenous., greedy, but Leonard always kept them away. But now they knew Leonard wasn't here. Or was it the man?

The man from the house on the road. He knew, too, and he breathed the same way heavy as the beasts. He wanted the baby and the thought startled her. The baby?

She had no baby. The men took the baby away. It was why they came. No wait a minute. the men hadn't taken the baby away, she had left the baby down by the pump, had put it on the ground. She had to go get the baby before the man got it but at the pump there was no baby. Gone back inside she saw the baby asleep in his little basket but she sweated from the panic. She had to look nice for Leonard.

◯ ◯ ◯

Soon they would bring Leonard. Yes. Yes. Now she saw the headlights. They wakened her fully awake. Oh how tired she had been but now she had her energy back. Run out to see. Out to the porch, out the door. Headlights, they're gone away. But they were there, that she knew.

She roamed in the house in the dark picking up things then putting them down, a slip of a thing in Tallahatta's overwhelming night, seeing things by starlight, sensing where familiar things were, pausing to coo over sleeping Leonard, junior. She changed a diaper.

And a little after two she rose from her second drowse, time to dress to go to town. Leonard would be back at any moment. Before the dresser mirror she removed her nightgown and looked at her body. What if they did take Leonard away and never did bring him back? "Never!" she shouted at the mirror. What would happen?

"Now, Frances," her mother told her as she fitted the wedding dress, "he will make his husbandly demands. You can cooperate but you don't have to enjoy it."

"I know, Mama, I know," Frances said.

"It's only nature acting out nature's way."

"I know."

But she did enjoy it. She took the feedsack dress from the dresser drawer.

Buttoned. "It's a powerful dress," she said to her image, giggling and giving the hips a wiggle. "Powerful dress. It's a powerful dress," That's what Leonard called it when she first put it on. "That was you, Mama," she said and twirled. "Maybe you didn't enjoy it, but I did, I'm me."

She pulled a chair in front of the mirror then sat and saw herself. That's me just like my wedding picture. Me sitting, him standing up tall behind me. A hand rested on her shoulder. "Husband and wife till death do us part." Now this Leonard in the mirror wore handcuffs, standing behind her, wild, wide-eyed.

"What God hath joined together let no man put asunder" she said to the handcuff image. The lamp became smoky now and she brought up the wick.

In the better light she said to the handcuffs "let no man put asunder."

Be serious now. Put it all behind you. Now for the baseball.

Frances had no baseball. The sugar bowl would have to do. It was round. The sugar was white. At the cupboard she took down the sugar and filled the bowl. It had to be completely filled.

Now with the lamp showing her in her feedsack dress she looked at Frances in the mirror. "Did you enjoy it, Mama? I did. I enjoyed it till everything else in the world went away and didn't matter, Mama, but tonight it matters, I grew up." Bad, bad, more than bad; evil, dresses, baseballs, the devil's game, and Tallahatta's nights, nights till death do us part.

Outside she could hear the noise now. Hear the stumps heaving themselves out of the ground to come help Frances.

"I don't need your help," she shouted to the stumps and they stopped.

She wound up, just as Leonard had shown her one time the way he wound up. The sugar bowl was the baseball and she saw the image of Frances in the lamplight. She threw. At her. The sugar bowl hit her image in the midsection and the mirror filled the room with a million shattered pieces flying into an instant constellation of glittering fragments of mirror and gleaming grains of sugar, a Milky Way in the dark lighted for an instant by the lamp and a beautiful sight to see. And to Frances, she herself had disappeared, just as she must do, as she wanted to do.

She lifted Leonard, junior, from his basket one more time, cradling him, rocking him in her arms

"Bye, baby bunting,"

She sang to him softly,

"Papa's gone a-hunting.
For to fetch a rabbit skin
To wrap his baby bunting in."
A rosy wisp of cloud to win
To wrap his baby bunting in

She lay Leonard, junior, back down..

Tired of life now, she stretched across the bed and smothered her face in the blanket. And she slept until six when Leonard, junior, woke and cooed and gurgled and woke her too, just as he always did.

SEVENTEEN

"WAS *WHAT?*" AARON SILVERSTEIN SAID into the telephone then listened for five minutes as Win Harrigan explained again the facts of Leonard's arrest.

"I'll be there tomorrow," he said. He hated the rusty bathtub at the little hotel over the drugstore. And he still didn't understand. He had shipped a Ford, delivered to him by the player named Buckles, to Chicago yesterday. In a crate. On a flatcar. Now there were *two* Model T Fords? Leonard Cassity driving around Thomasville in a shiny new Model T Ford?

○ ○ ○

"He can't come to trial."

"No."

"It won't take much police work to figure this out."

"No," Win Harrigan agreed again.

"What about his wife?" Silverstein asked. "Does she know?"

"I think not. She's an upstanding girl. Good family. He parades her around Thomasville in it. She doesn't know." Aaron Silverstein groaned.

Win Harrigan brought out a bottle of Bourbon whiskey; the two talked on.

"Why would he take a car belonging to the vice president of the Mobile and Ohio Railroad of all people?" Silverstein said. "Now he's raising hell all over the state of Mississippi. They have this new agency they call the Mississippi Bureau of Theft that's anxious to make a name for itself and some beloved war hero with a bum leg from the war and a nose for crime like Sherlock Holmes is prowling around. Has a witness."

Win Harrigan groaned. "He didn't know whose car it was."

Finally Silverstein said "I have a plan."

It did have its appeals, Win agreed.

"We have to keep his picture out of the paper," Silverstein went on. "That's important. And he can't come to trial."

"No."

"Comiskey's scout came to see me after he found out who I was. He'll pay ten thousand for him."

"Still?"

"Still. We'll change his name. Comiskey will go along."

"Pay for a convict?"

"No. We'll bust him out. A year in semi-pro ball in Texas to let the heat cool down and then Comiskey brings him up as Victor Laredo or somebody. New identity. His wife has to help."

"Victor Laredo?"

"Or somebody. Comiskey's desperate to rebuild the Sox. Ten thousand isn't much. And if his picture's never been in the paper there's nothing to recognize."

"But what about the M&O man?"

"Gets a new car. And better."

"The witness?"

"The colored man who cleans up the grounds? He's the witness."

"Him."

"He suddenly won't remember exactly. Have a bad memory. We'll use what we call the Chicago Technique."

"I'm not familiar."

"Bribe them or bury them, either works. You say you can get the items. Put that in motion. In my opinion, it's going to be duck soup."

Those times in his career he had had to tell a widow there was no insurance, he had seen the same reaction: tortured, vacant, tearless silence. "...stopped paying the premiums some time back. I guess he forgot to tell you."

She and Win Harrigan sat at Frances' dining room table. Frances had put out some sugar cookies on a plate. Now the confidence Win Harrigan felt a day ago had left him. He had been through the times when he had had to tell a widow the insurance had lapsed, but this held a difference. He studied Frances' face, young, tired, and old.

"... and they will put him on what they call Parchman Farm. It's out in the Delta. He'll hoe cotton all day and wear convict stripes. A man on a horse and with a shotgun rides around like an overseer. And that's what he is, an overseer. It's like slavery days. No, it is slavery. It's no different.

"If you want to see him you'll have to go to Jackson and catch what they call the Midnight Special. It leaves at midnight every Saturday for your day of visit on Sunday."

Frances looked at the plate of cookies, absently, and then she broke one in half and pushed the larger half to Win Harrigan.

Never as a little girl had she cried. When she bumped her head so bad; when she scraped her knee. She just sniffed her nose and held her head up straight. Never since the accident had she grieved aloud, not even to Fergie. These words now were all the voice of her grief that there ever were or ever would be. Despite the gray cheeks and the deep, tired eyes, the dry words came out from far back inside her in a voice level and calm.

"I lost my father, you know."

"I know," said Win Harrigan.

"I can't lose Leonard, too."

Frances agreed to help break her husband Leonard Cassity out of jail.

EIGHTEEN

Aᴀᴛᴇʀ ʜᴇ ʜᴀᴅ ᴄʟᴏsᴇᴅ ᴛʜᴇ office for the day Win Harrigan poured himself a glass of Bourbon whiskey then opened the box Doctor Pearlington had received from the medical supply house in Montgomery. Everything he asked for had arrived. The warm night and the warming Bourbon let him think, about the reasons he had left his native Kentucky and opened this insurance agency far from home. He had been a young man seeking a challenge. Win Harrigan knew how to drink Bourbon, slow sips accompanied by contemplation. Prohibition had not yet reached Kentucky and his people at home kept him supplied, kept him in contact with home.

It seemed a good idea, a baseball team, and his suggestion earned him chairmanship of the town booster committee. He put the team together and it had been a good thing for Thomasville. It gave them community pride. What if he had cut a few corners? That was all behind the scenes. When the roads came through it would all have been worth while. He couldn't lose sight of that. He let out a long breath.

But he couldn't meditate on civic pride tonight. He had to concentrate on the details of breaking Leonard out of jail tomorrow. The circuit judge would arrive in two days.

He thought an early evening arrival would be best. Sometimes the Bible-thumpers came to the jail to preach to the captives behind bars and he wanted to wait until they would be at home having their suppers. The prisoners of course didn't take their salvation without protest and the deputy had to stay around threatening them for cursing the preachers. The commotion died down around seven. Absently, he reached into the desk and took out a pair of steel-rimmed glasses. They belonged to a client who left them behind one day then died the next. He had always intended to return them to the widow, but now he tried them on in front of the bathroom mirror. They added to his appearance and made him look professional. *You never know, do you?* He asked himself. *You never know.*

Shortly after twelve the next day Win Harrigan rolled to a stop under the oak in front of the house at Tallahatta Springs. "I'll just be a few minutes," said Frances and she took the package Win Harrigan handed her. "Watch the baby". Frances lay Leonard, junior, in his basket across the back seat.

Ten minutes later the most beautiful nurse Win Harrigan had ever seen emerged, a comely young woman in a long navy blue skirt with a white apron and a white starched cap pinned high on her head. A short navy blue cape lined in crimson had been buttoned across her chest. Win Harrigan had never before seen such a change. Frances sat in the seat next to him. "Drive," she said.

Around six-thirty the two parked a block from the Clarke County jail and Frances unpacked the sandwiches she had made. They watched the front door. All quiet.

At five to seven they pulled to the front door. Win Harrigan stepped out. Off the back seat he took a black kit, the kind physicians carry, which he opened to check its contents. He had a similar kit for Frances, a little smaller. From his own kit he removed a small revolver and he transferred it into Frances kit then closed both. Next he put on the eyeglasses his client had left behind, finally he draped a stethoscope across his neck. The doctor and his nurse went into the jail.

A young man in a brown uniform sat at the desk inside. He seemed neither asleep nor awake.

"Are you holding someone named Leonard Cassity?" Win Harrigan asked.

The deputy looked at the pair. "Holding? You mean Leonard? Holding him tighter than a sardine in a can. Who are you?"

"I am Doctor Lee and this is Nurse Hodges. I am treating Mister Cassity for a stomach ailment and I have to examine him."

"You mean his bellyache?"

"You know?"

"You couldn't not know, listening to him."

"Have you given him anything?"

"We don't give people much around here."

"It's very important I see him."

"I'll take you down there."

"Here, please," said Doctor Lee. "I have to lay him across a table with his legs spread wide. Your desk will do."

"I think I need to call somebody about this."

"Please, deputy," said Frances.

"You see," said Doctor Lee. "This woman is trained to give care, a calling she practiced on the Western Front."

"I think I need to call."

"Hmmnn," said Doctor Lee. "It occurs to me that you need the examination, too. It's performed with a surgical glove, a finger and some Vaseline. Have you had it?"

"No."

"Stick out your tongue. Yes, you need the exam. Drop your pants and lean over the desk. I'll go and get Leonard."

"Drop my pants? There's a lady here,"

"It doesn't matter. She's a professional. Duty on the Western Front, remember? We're taking Leonard". Somehow the words came out as sort of a boast. Where are the keys?" Stretched over the desk the deputy pointed. "In that cabinet."

Doctor Lee went through the rear door and came back with a tired-looking, disheveled Leonard in jail stripes.

Leonard looked at the deputy draped across the desk and Frances in the nurse uniform and said "Frances?"

"Who?" asked the deputy.

"Frances, my wife," said Leonard.

"I'm going to call," said the deputy. "This is a jailbreak."

"Yes it is," said Doctor Lee, "a good one. Frances, take this." Doctor Lee opened Frances' bag, fishing out the little revolver. "Leonard has to change."

"I'm calling. I want the phone," said the deputy again and struggled upward.

"Stay still," said Frances. "If you move I'll shoot….shoot your balls." Frances aimed the revolver.

"Frances," said Leonard, "you're not supposed to talk about somebody's balls."

"The Western Front," reminded Doctor Lee. "Balls wounds are among the worst."

"Oh, goddam," said the deputy. "*I* was on the Western Front."

"Change, Leonard," said Doctor Lee.

NINETEEN

Dear Mother Cassity

<u>You must send me bus fare to Mobile!</u> It is $3.25. A baby in arms rides free. Send it to me care of General Delivery here at Hamilton. Use the name I have written on the enclosed slip of paper and I will ask for it that way. But if somebody asks you where I am you don't know. . When Mister Harrigan give me that pistol he did not tell me he had pulled the hammer back. I got flustered and it went off. I won't tell you where it hit him but I will tell you he won't be any good for a woman any more. All that has happened should not happen to a dog. <u>Should not happen to a dog!</u> I always get put in the middle of things. I will tell you all the details later but this much I must tell you now.

I am a widow!

With more love than you will Know
Frances Cassity

At the station look for someone dressed up like a nurse. Will explain.

○ ○ ○

Win Harrigan brushed past the spread-out deputy as he went into the back room that held the cells, a row of three down the back wall. Leonard occupied the middle cell. Clarke County had no other prisoners at the moment.

On his way he had seen a door which opened to the outside and thought momentarily of locking it, then decided it wasn't worth the time. Now, as he heard the door open and close he knew he had made a mistake. Win Harrigan opened the physician's bag and, removed a US Army Colt .45 in a holster and unbuttoned the flap... Whoever it was would see the open door to Leonard's cell.

"Say, Ralph, why…" said a voice and a middle-aged man in a deputy's uniform came into the room. "Jailbreak!" shouted the deputy lying across the desk.

"Jailbreak! Oh no, you don't!" the new deputy shouted back and he began to fumble for his holster. "It's a jailbreak, Tom," the new deputy said to the deputy who lay across the desk.

"Goddamit, I know that," said the deputy. "I told *you*."

"Hands up," commanded the new deputy even though he had trouble locating his weapon which had slewed toward the back of his hip. "Keep your man still, Frances," he said.

The prone deputy began to fumble for his trousers.

"I mean this," said Frances.

"Frances, stop this mess." Leonard spoke. "I'll take off my pants and go back to my cell."

"Oh, no, you won't," said Win Harrigan.

"No, Leonard, you won't," said Frances

"Shoot them," the deputy lying on the desk called to the new deputy. But the new deputy had ducked behind the door to the cells. All Win Harrigan could see was a revolver in a shaky hand pointing through the doorway. Win Harrigan thought he saw the deputy fire, but knew the bullet must have gone into the floor.

Frances heard a sound. "Oh, no," she said and realized the pop she heard had come from her own revolver. It must have gone off. She knew she'd gotten nervous. She must have squeezed the trigger. "Oh, no," she said again and the deputy groaned. "Oh, no. I didn't mean to," Frances told the deputy. "I didn't mean it. I'm sorry."

"Keep shooting," said Win Harrigan, and the deputy fired again from behind the door.

"Her, not you," shouted Win Harrigan.

Win Harrigan fired again, this time at the single light bulb. The bulb shattered and the room became black. In the dark Win Harrigan fired again. The deputy behind the door fired into the room. Now in the dark flashes seemed to come from everywhere. Maybe the deputy lying on the desk had found his weapon. Flashes brought little moments of light into the room. "Move to the door," shouted Win Harrigan. Frances fired again. "Call me a doctor," yelled the wounded deputy. In the dark Frances moved toward the door. "Quick, Leonard." She fell across something in the dark. She had stumbled over Leonard. He must have fallen... "Give me your hand," and when Leonard held out his hand to Frances it felt wet. "Oh, Frances," said Leonard.

In the next second the room became silent and black. Frances threw her pistol on the floor. "Everybody," she said. "Everybody."

Outside the town lay silent and still. A town that had retired for the evening to its own affairs dark and sleepy. No one seemed to have known that a gun battle had taken place.

They had left the engine running.

"Drive, Leonard," said Win Harrigan. He seemed to be dragging a leg. "I may be hurt." He half-stumbled then caught himself.

"I'll help," said Frances. Win Harrigan grasped a leg. "It's right here."

"I've got a feeling in my stomach, Frances," said Leonard, "it aches. It's a pain, too."

"You drive, Frances," said Win Harrigan.

"I can't," Frances said.

"You have to find me a doctor."

"We have to go back..."

"Get me there," said Win Harrigan.

"Me, too," said Leonard.

Frances opened a door for Win Harrigan. "Get in next to the baby," she said. "Leonard, next to me."

Frances, fifteen minutes ago "Nurse Hodge" slid behind the wheel.

She tried to jam the car into gear and heard a grinding sound. "The clutch," said Win Harrigan. "Clutch it." The words came out in a gasp.

Frances pressed the clutch then pushed the gearshift lever. The car bucked and lurched but it moved forward. "Shift it now," said Win Harrigan. Leonard's hand came over and resting on hers over the gearshift. "Clutch," he said and shifted the car into another gear. Frances at last had gained command of the steering wheel and she followed the streetlights to the road north. In the dark she heard some choking sounds but she had no idea who made them. "Lights," said Leonard. She had not turned on the headlights. She had almost left the road. "Be fair to me, God," she said to herself then said to Leonard "I'm taking us home, dear," and she did not know if God or Leonard had heard her or not.

Now on the road north she could feel the dampness on her apron. For a moment she turned her head backward and saw that Win Harrigan had grown limp. Leonard, junior, lay in his basket and Win Harrigan, she knew, had no need of a doctor.

Leonard on the other hand held onto his life.

In a quarter of an hour they would reach Thomasville. But Thomasville, she knew, would be only a stop on the way to prison. Prison now for her, too. *Orphans have no chance,* she thought. The thought that she would keep Leonard, junior, away from the orphanage calmed her. She had to keep that life away from him. Keep it at a distance. Only that. She had to.

Beyond Thomasville would be Demopolis. "Be fair to me, God," she prayed it now. "Be fair. In Jesus' name, amen."

She looked at Leonard. "I have nothing I can give to you dear. No medicine."

She drove through the town and north of Thomasville Leonard said weakly "my belly, Frances, like a bellyache."

"You have bellyaches, remember, dear you always have bellyaches."

"I remember."

A few minutes later Leonard said "Frances?"

"What, dear?"

"I've made mistakes."

"What mistakes, dear?"

"I don't know. Just mistakes."

"You've made no mistakes, dear. None. Never."

"Oh."

"Frances?"

"Dear?"

"Our first kiss. Was it vanilla? Or chocolate?

"Chocolate, dear."

Frances could feel Leonard tremble in the seat next to her. She rested a hand on his, wet in the dark with something she could not see.

"Frances," said Leonard, "he's coming for me."

"Who's coming for you, dear?"

"The Holy Ghost. I can see the fire of him."

"He baptizes in fire and water. You are being baptized by the Holy Ghost, that's all dear. Just baptized."

"Umn," said Leonard, the final sound he ever made in his life.

She drove and she realized that only she and her son had survived this night. But the dull realization offered nothing to her, no hope. The dashboard had a clock and it read sometime after two in the morning and she kept along the road to Demopolis. How could those old tree stumps live in that kind of darkness out there, she thought. It was too black. At home she had light. Now she saw that something lay ahead in the darkness. Ahead she saw a bridge.

This was a long, wooden bridge with steel rails. The headlights picked up the far end. A bridge, what of it? She asked herself, slowing. She stopped the car.

With the headlights to light her Frances walked out to the middle of the bridge. The stream lay about twenty below, almost as dark as the rest of the night, but holding tiny reflections from the headlights. She walked to the end.

At the far end of the bridge there seemed to be a track or a crude road that turned right off the shoulder. Cars had been there.... The track led down the embankment and she knew the track led to a place where people came to fish under the bridge, or to commit adultery. Tonight it had a new purpose and she looked back at the headlights.

"You are fair, aren't you, God?" she said and walked back to the car.

Slowly she drove across then turned off the shoulder. She edged the car down the embankment then stopped it under the bridge. The stream looked twenty feet wide and deep. Deep enough, she hoped.

Now she had to get Leonard, junior, out. She placed him on the ground. What a good sleeper, he was, Frances thought. That has always been a blessing. But, she thought, what if he wakes and cries and is hungry? I'll just feed him and change him. There's no one here. This place will always be just like this.

Frances made her goodbyes. For an hour she sat, on the running board or in the driver's seat; sometimes stroking Leonard's limp hand. "I fell in love with you the first day, but I wouldn't tell you," she said. "You can play baseball, dear. Why should I give a hoot? You were good, did you know that? I knew that. And you know that car? I didn't want it. Not really. You were everything. I have to say goodbye to you now, Leonard. You know that this that I am doing makes our son to grow up strong and good. He will always owe this to his father. Goodbye."

She started the car. If she could give it enough momentum it would sail into the center of the stream. She wanted it to reach midstream. She said to Leonard and to Mister Harrigan "it's the only way." She would have to back the car up.

In the light of the dashboard she thought that Leonard stared at her. "Chocolate, dear," she said for the last time. "You couldn't ever remember it right. But it was good being children together, wasn't it? Tonight we grew up."

Frances put the car into gear and pressed the gas pedal. She let out the clutch. This was her smoothest start and the car gained speed faster than she thought. "Out!" she said aloud and flung herself out the door onto the ground. She watched the car travel its last fifteen feet.

The car hurtled over the creek bank then tilted into the stream throwing up water. She saw the headlights disappear into the dark and then all the blackness of the night had come back. She had done it and only the darkness of night had seen what she had done.

Demopolis lay up the road and she trudged. She did not know how far she would have to walk.

Up the road, exchanging the heavy basket for the light one from arm to arm It must be about the time Leonard, junior, would wake and demand his bottle and a change of diapers. Finally, Leonard, junior, woke. "I don't think I'll ever sleep again," she said to him and he gurgled. "Time you had some carrots." and she sat him down.

Leonard's basket had grown heavy now. And in the now growing light she made something out, a sign, and it said "Demopolis."

"I'm exhausted, God," Frances said. "Are we here?"

In the growing light Frances could make out shapes. Houses ahead. A building had a tall white steeple. Church.

Next to the church Frances could make out a house, a brick house, like the church was brick. And from the house, a light, someone would be up.

Frances walked to the door and took a final look at herself. Her white apron had become spattered with blood. She had wiped her bloody hand on it. She straightened her cap and tucked the blanket around Leonard, junior. This was the best she could do. Ready now, Frances? Now knock. She knocked.

Frances heard a sound, a stirring inside. Someone had heard the knock. She took a deep breath. How would she ever find a thing to say?

The door opened. Frances saw a woman, an older woman. She wore a heavy bathrobe. She must have been her mother's age or even a few years older. Frances looked at a face, puzzled, but other than that, kindly.

"Lord, child," said the woman, "who in the world are you?"

EPILOGUE

January 12, 1943

Dear Mother,

I am sorry to leave you with only this note of
goodbye. But I know you would have persuaded me to
stay. I wanted to stay until after Christmas. Our
country needs me and many others right now and I
am on the bus to Camp Shelby, Miss., where I will
be inducted into the United States Army. You have
raised me by yourself these 22 years and you took
the plainest kind of jobs. But I want you to know you
looked beautiful to me in your waitress uniforms and I
was always proud of you. After basic I will get some
leave and I will be home to see you and give you a
proper goodbye.

I love you,

Leonard, Junior

PHIL BRADY

v-mail

France,
12 June, 1944

Dear Mother,

We came ashore on the beach the other day and I tell
you I have never seen anything like it before in my
life and I hope I never will again. But I am okay.

Love, Leonard

Belgium
30 January, 1945

Dear Mrs. Cassity,

I want to write to you to tell you of the circumstances of the death in action of your son, Leonard.

We had to establish a machine gun position which had to be held to allow our company to withdraw. I could not order a soldier to this duty and I asked for a volunteer. Leonard was that volunteer. Frankly I do not know what instills in our young men the kind of bravery they exhibit over here, but in the case of Leonard Cassity, Junior, I rather suspect that you had something to do with it. I would like you to know that because of your son, dozens of young men have survived to fight another day and dozens of mothers have received a comfort that sadly I wish you could have.

Leonard of course will receive the Purple Heart. It is a beautiful medal in the shape of a heart with a bust of George Washington on a field of purple. You should treasure it. But in addition I have also recommended Corporal Leonard Cassity, Junior, for the Silver Star for his gallantry in action on 25 December, 1944, at Bastogne, Belgium.

Mrs. Cassity, somewhere there is a Creator Who welcomes young men like Leonard to His bosom and Who honors their names eternally. You may be assured that that is where Leonard is.

Sincerely,

Thomas Heaston Bramlett
Lt. Col., United States Army

1 September, 1945
Troopship President Chester A. Arthur

Dear Mother,

Please don't reply to this letter because I will
probably be home before it would reach me. I am being
separated from the United States Army Air Force in
New York next week and I will spend a few days there
visiting with Dad's relatives. Then I am bound for
home. I will have a few photos of me and my buddies to
show you. But that's all history now.

Did I ever tell you I had the name of Dad's old
baseball team painted on the cowling of my P-51? I had
a big baseball with the name "Clarke County Democrats"
painted across it. It looked great.

Sometimes I wonder what those German pilots would
have thought if they knew that it was an American Jew
behind them firing those tracer bullets! I got one or
two but others got more than I did.

Mother, you know I will have to look for a job, don't
you? Do you think you could find me a spot at the bank?
Not a position, just a job. But you would think a
degree in business from the University of Alabama would
be worth something.

Right now I am looking at the skyline of New York. It
looks wonderful. Soon I will knock at your door. Put
out the welcome mat.

Your son,

Francis X. "Frank" Silverstein
Soon to be ex-Captain, United States Army Air Force

It took her a long time to find the courage to make the trip. She had no car. She had to borrow a car. She could borrow Gus the manager's car, she had done that before, on a pretext, saying she would be back in an hour. She asked and Gus of course said yes. She took off her apron.

All the way north her hand rested on the King James Version of the Bible. Gus wouldn't conclude that his car had been stolen for hours maybe. She relaxed a little and drove.

Through and past the two towns, Grove Hill and Thomasville, the town where she was raised, her girlhood home. The past she had been forced to forget. Her life. The long sacrifice of what had been her life. Her moment when she first saw Leonard in the store. How could all that have come to this?

But she was brave. She had raised a young man who had decided to put himself into the Army where he had put others above himself, whose letters were short and innocent, without any crime or wrongdoing, without mistakes and full of courage.

His medals would arrive one day soon and she believed they would be sent back marked "addressee unknown." This was a hard trip to make.

Closer now to Demopolis, it was funny how it all came back to her. The main road and then the little side path. There it was. Still there. Again she stopped, just like before, then she made the car buck and rumble over the underbrush. She knew there had to be a car out there somewhere. Somewhere at the bottom. And in the car, two bodies. Mister Harrigan, the owner and playing manager, and Leonard Cassity, her husband, pitcher for the Clarke County Democrats. There for 23 years.

Frances opened her Bible to the Book of Ruth to Chapter One Verse 16. "Do not ask me to abandon or forsake you. For wherever you go I will go. Wherever you lodge I will lodge, your people shall be my people and your God my God. Wherever you die I will die and there shall I be buried beside you.… If aught but death separate me from you." So long ago she had pledged this kind of loyalty. She thought. *I shall be buried beside you.* She stared at the steam. *In just a few moments from now.*

But was this loyalty? To be loyal was the promise she had made to herself so many times over her life. *But now?* She did not know. Somehow Leonard, Junior, had made her better than she was; better than she was supposed to be. *Had that not been loyalty?* Neither her husband…nor her son…would expect….her to do this. Finally, she spoke. She said "I didn't really want the car, Leonard," and she turned to make the long drive back to Mobile.

AUTHOR'S NOTE

THE DECADES THROUGHOUT THE TWENTIETH Century when baseball was at its zenith as the national pastime are today only dimly seen. They can be seen as records in record books piled somewhere upon dusty record books. As players, names, seen through modern eyes, mythical figures who wore shortish pants atop long wooly stockings playing with stubby-fingered gloves who used ungainly bats to compile incredulous batting averages, and who played without rest only in the daytime. performing larger than life roles on larger than life stages—and showing themselves as also gifted by tragic flaw.

With the Democrats I have written the novel I have always wanted to write about baseball. Also, it is a novel about life and love, about a young semi-pro pitcher for a team in a small Alabama town in the early 1920's. It is about him and his young wife and their separate routes to change.

This country in the early 1920's was a country full of energy and vitality and youthful growth. The Great War in Europe, called "The War to End All Wars," had arrived at a cessation of hostilities, The Armistice. America stood an ocean away from all that. America had energy and those new things of pleasure: the automobile, the phonograph to play music, bands to dance by, the movies and their stars, Prohibition and bootlegging and gangsters; speakeasies, and the womans' vote, radios, the telephone. America basked in the joy of comforts of living and and the crash and Depression that would come in 1929 was unthinkable in the early 1920's.

America also had its dark side. Prejudice, discrimination against Negroes, Jews, Catholics, not only prevailed in different degrees in different regions, but discrimination could also govern everyday life and politics. Gambling and corruption entered sport, and not just baseball. Prizefighting and fixed fights weren't uncommon.

"The Clarke County Democrats" follows on the Black Sox scandal of 1919. The fixed World Series of that year and it fits into it. But it comments on what I thought of that generation which gave birth to "The Greatest Generation" and what that generation was like. If they uniquely gave birth to the Greatest Generation, their uniqueness was that they were not unique at all and this is a tricky point to make.

Some parts of the Democrats and some of the characters even may infringe on today's efforts to smooth out the past, but to leave out the attitudes and the stereotyping that played roles in the sport of baseball in the 1920's is to deprive the game of people who surrounded the game and gave it a flavor and color that no other sport has ever had in any other time. But all the characters are American; they can and do act, variously, in an American way.